A First Date with Death

"Loved it! Daring, funny, and unforgettable, Georgia is a protagonist you'll identify with. Dreamy men, romance, and a plot that twists to the end. I was drawn in by the memorable characters and a glimpse into the crazy world of 'reality' television."

—Nancy J. Parra, author of the Perfect Proposals Mysteries and the Baker's Treat Mysteries

"A great vicarious adventure . . . Diana has a hit with this new series! I highly recommend this novel [to readers who] enjoy well-written cozy mysteries with more than a little bit of romance, strong female characters, humor, and a challenge."

—Open Book Society

PRAISE FOR
DIANA ORGAIN'S OTHER NOVELS

"Fast-paced and fun."

—Rhys Bowen, *New York Times* bestselling author

"Stellar . . . A winning protagonist and a glorious San Francisco setting . . . Highly recommended."

—Sheldon Siegel, *New York Times* bestselling author

"A fantastically fun read . . . Not only offers humor and suspense, but also makes sure to not solve the puzzle until the last pages."

—*Suspense Magazine*

"An over-the-top good-time cozy mystery. With a feisty heroine and with lots of humor, plenty of intrigue and suspense . . . this novel is a delightful treat to read."

—*Fresh Fiction*

Berkley Prime Crime Titles by Diana Orgain

Third Time's a Crime

DIANA ORGAIN

BERKLEY PRIME CRIME
New York

BERKLEY PRIME CRIME
Published by Berkley
An imprint of Penguin Random House LLC
375 Hudson Street, New York, New York 10014

Copyright © 2017 by Diana Orgain
Penguin Random House supports copyright. Copyright fuels creativity, encourages
diverse voices, promotes free speech, and creates a vibrant culture. Thank you for buying
an authorized edition of this book and for complying with copyright laws by not
reproducing, scanning, or distributing any part of it in any form without permission.
You are supporting writers and allowing Penguin Random House to continue to
publish books for every reader.

BERKLEY is a registered trademark and BERKLEY PRIME CRIME and the B colophon
are trademarks of Penguin Random House LLC.

ISBN: 9780425271704

First Edition: January 2017

Printed in the United States of America
1   3   5   7   9   10   8   6   4   2

Cover art by Bill Bruning
Cover design by Danielle Mazzella di Bosco
Book design by Laura K. Corless

For Tom Sr., Carmen, Tommy, and Bobby,
my own special tribe!

Acknowledgments

· ·

Thank you to my wonderful editor, Michelle Vega, and the entire crew over at Berkley Prime Crime for making this a better book. Thanks to my superagent, Jill Marsal, for your never-ending enthusiasm and support.

Special thanks to my dear friend Marina Adair—your insights give me the courage to listen to my heart.

Thanks to all my early readers, especially Chrystal Carver— you keep me on track.

Extra thanks to Kirsten Weiss for the haunted castle tour, the ghostly plot brainstorming, and all the fun!

Shout-out and hugs to my Carmen, Tommy, Bobby, and Tom Sr.—love you all!

Finally, thank you to all the dear readers who have written to me. Your kind words keep me motivated to write the next story.

One

....

The raven swept down upon us in a terrifying plunge, talons outstretched, screeching at an ear-shattering pitch. Instinctively, I jumped out of the way and reached for my gun, only remembering too late that I hadn't carried one in eighteen months, since I'd been let go from the San Francisco Police Department.

The bird's massive wings flapped so close to me that the breeze lifted my hair, and I fought the urge to strike out at it. Suddenly, the bird arched up and flew to the top point of the castle, perching itself overhead.

The woman next to me gasped. "A raven? That's a bad omen."

Cheryl Dennison, our executive producer, yelled, "Did you all catch that?"

"I got it," one of the cameramen shouted excitedly. "I got a great shot."

"Good," Cheryl said, a self-satisfied smile playing on her face. "We'll want to use that in the promos."

"Cheryl probably shipped that bird in from Hollywood," I said under my breath to the woman next to me. "Just to capture that shot."

The woman, a former FBI profiler, made a face. As if she disapproved of Hollywood histrionics.

We were on location at the Golden Castle, said to be haunted and the scene of an unsolved murder. During its heyday, it'd doubled as a reform school. It stood nestled on the hill overlooking the charming old mining town of Golden, California. But the castle was far from charming. It was so large it blotted out the sun and the windows were dark and murky. The exterior bricks had been built in San Quentin Prison and they projected a feeling of doom and gloom. Overall, the castle had such an ominous presence that it screamed "horror film," or in our case, "bad reality TV."

My best friend and the assistant producer, Becca, had begged me for weeks to accept the casting offer. She knew I wasn't too keen on the paranormal aspect of the show. I wasn't exactly a "believer" but now, despite myself, looking at the castle sent a shiver up my spine. I squeezed Scott's hand as we hiked up the gravel driveway toward it.

"All right!" Scott said, barely able to keep the excitement out of his voice. "It's downright menacing."

I giggled. I knew that, being a horror writer, this haunted castle was right up his alley.

"Remind me again why I'm doing this?" I asked.

"To solve the crime," he said.

"The fact that this is my third stint on reality TV *is* the crime," I said.

Scott flashed me his winning smile, reminding me again why I always felt so warm and happy in his presence.

We'd met and fallen in love on the first show, and won the cash prize to boot. However, the money hadn't stretched as far as we'd hoped and we'd signed up for the whole rodeo again. But the second time, I hadn't won the money, and after starring on reality TV, my chances of ever landing a job as a police officer again were between slim and none.

I figured I better take the opportunity to solve a case while I could. Who knew, maybe I'd be able to salvage a shred of my reputation.

Beside us, the famous forensic archaeologist from the *Hunting Bones* reality show chuckled. "You know you love it," he said.

I turned to him. "Love what? Solving a crime?"

He glanced over at Scott and was seemingly deciding if he should say what was really on his mind. When he noticed that Scott was mesmerized by the castle looming over us, he said, "The limelight."

"You don't seem to mind it yourself," I said, trying my best not to bristle.

He was tall with piercing blue eyes and a confidence that made him handsome. He had the type of square jaw and prominent nose that was extremely photogenic. I knew without a doubt his looks were the reason that *Hunting Bones* had been such a smashing success.

"All right, listen up, folks," Cheryl said. "As you know, we need to get some final images for the intro montage, so please line up over here where the light is best and let's get some usable footage before we get on to filming the first episode."

A rumble of excitement worked its way through the cast and crew. We were quite a crowd. On location, there were ten of us contestants, the show's host, Harris Carlson, several cameramen, lighting techs, sound techs, the hair and makeup folks, along with the production team.

The cast took turns lining up against the awful red bricks; preening, primping, and pirouetting on Cheryl's request.

We were five teams of two players. Scott and I made up one team. Dr. Arch, the forensic archaeologist, and his sometimes cohost, the FBI profiler Karen Kenley, made up the second team. There was a historian from an Ivy League college paired with her brother, a priest. Then a professed ghost hunter partnered with a psychic. And finally two young women, the castle docent and the unsolved murder victim's great niece.

Our mission was to solve the murder of Jane Reiner. According to the limited information we'd been given, the historical accounts about Jane's murder all differed.

Some said she'd been hung in the kitchen, other accounts claimed she'd been stabbed in the basement, and still others said she'd been shot in the supply room.

All accounts seemed to believe that Jane haunted the castle and would continue to do so until her murder could be solved. Rumor had it that she appeared from time to time to visitors either hanging in the kitchen or bleeding in the basement or supply rooms.

None of the information squared, so in Cheryl's infinite wisdom, she'd pitched to a Hollywood Studio the idea that a team of misfits might be able to solve the historic murder on national television.

Needless to say, it was such a bad idea that Hollywood loved it.

Once inside the castle, the creep factor only escalated. The inside of the building was like a maze with steps and hallways spinning in every direction, vertically and horizontally. The stairs were worn and creaked as the cast and crew climbed them to what was known as the prayer room.

A strange smell filled the room, like sulfur mixed with stale kerosene that someone had attempted to mask with a flowery perfume.

"Whoa! Do you smell that?" the psychic asked. "It's a presence! Most certainly a presence!"

The man claiming to be a psychic was the least likely person I would have expected. I figured Cheryl would have cast a pretty blond young lady, but instead the man before us was as large as a lumberjack, complete with a burly red beard. I'd liked him immediately, even though, of course, I couldn't believe a word he uttered.

I wrinkled my nose. "I think the room's probably been closed up a long time."

"No, no," the docent disagreed. She worked at the Golden Castle as one of the tour guides. "We air it out every day, but the smell always returns."

Fingers tickled the back of my neck and I involuntarily jumped as Scott leaned in close to me, his lips touching my ear. "Oooh," he whispered. "Creeeeeppppy."

"I thought you were here to protect me, not freak me out," I said.

He pressed his forehead to mine, looking into my eyes. "You certainly don't need my protection, but you have it, babe, always."

As Scott leaned in to kiss me, Cheryl's screechy voice interrupted our romantic moment. "People! Listen up. The team is going to need a few minutes here to set up the cameras, lights, and mikes. We'll kick off the show here. Harris will give the introduction. The camera will pan on each of you as Harris introduces you. Then we'll go ahead and start the castle tour for the viewers. You'll all need to make sure your hair and makeup are set. Please don't wander off and get lost."

Scott rubbed at his shaved head. "I'd better see to getting my hair fixed."

"It is kind of messy," I joked. Suddenly, I had the

strange sensation of being watched. Which one would think I'd be used to after two tours of reality TV; nevertheless I still found the feeling mildly disconcerting. I turned to find Dr. Arch staring at Scott and me.

"You two don't seem to be taking this very seriously," he said.

Scott hid his amusement. "You believe in all the hocus-pocus going on here, doctor? Spirits trapped in the in between."

The priest, who'd been meditating in front of a candle, snapped to attention. "Oh, I do think there is evil here. With much prayer, we can send the spirits on."

Cheryl strode between us. "Now, now, father. We had this discussion, didn't we? Save it for the cameras." The priest shook his head and seemed ready to argue, but Cheryl was already on to the next group, calling out, "Five minutes, people. Ready in five."

"Anyway, what I meant," Dr. Arch continued, "is that you have to take this one seriously. It's viewer determined, you know. If you don't get the votes, you'll be sent packing. Even though I'm betting against myself here for a moment, I think you two probably have the best chance of solving the mystery."

Dr. Arch's partner, Karen Kenley, sidled up to him. "That's some vote of confidence, Arch."

The doctor looked chagrined. "I didn't mean anything against you, honey."

Karen Kenley, the FBI profiler, looked like the type of woman who never accepted any excuse, either from a man or much less from a woman. Her straight black hair hung like a curtain around her face. She had the type of sharp features that let you know right away if you messed with her, you'd get cut.

Cheryl clapped her hands again. "Okay, people," she shouted. "Places please. Cast, line up here." She indicated a row of blue painter's tape the crew had laid down for us. "Harris, you'll stand here—" A large thump against one of the windows startled Cheryl. She put a hand over her heart. "What was that?"

"A bird, I think," Scott said. He rushed to the window, but the glass was so hazy it was impossible to see through.

The lumberjack psychic next to me moaned and pressed his fingers to his temple.

His partner, the ghost hunter, fiddled with a device strapped to his belt and asked, "Can we go outside and take a look? I have to investigate. My EMF is going crazy."

"What's that?" Scott asked.

"It measures fluctuations in the electromagnetic fields," he said.

Cheryl collected herself. "Let's not get distracted here, folks. We have to start filming." She put on a headset and made a beeline to the back of the set and motioned for the cameras to start rolling.

Harris took center stage and said directly into the camera, "Welcome, America, to *Cold Case in the Castle*!" Harris's voice boomed in his made-for-TV persona. "We're coming to you from Golden, California, where the town has had a dark and tragic unsolved mystery haunting them since 1968. You see, back in the early 1900s this castle was a reform school, a home for the state's most delinquent wards. However good-intentioned the state may have been in wishing to rehabilitate the wards, horrors came to pass: abuses, escape attempts, violent encounters, inhumane punishments, and, yes, ladies and gentlemen, even murder."

Harris gave a dramatic pause, then continued. "There were five murders that took place on these grounds. All were solved." Harris held up his index finger and gave a flourish as he said, "Except for one.

"The disturbing and brutal murder of Jane Reiner. Jane had been an innocent and lovely youth, working as a librarian in training, when she mysteriously disappeared. Her body was later discovered heinously murdered on the premises of the reform school."

The cast made the appropriate gasps and tsking sounds.

Harris launched into a brief recap of the facts we'd been given, then said, "And that's where you, dear viewer, come in." Harris continued, "Join us, as we travel back in time and solve Jane's murder. We've assembled a cast that we believe can help us do just that."

One by one, he motioned toward us and introduced the cast. When he finally landed on the last contestant, the lumberjack psychic suddenly moaned as if in pain and fell to his knees. He screamed out, "Oh, no!"

"Oh, brother," I mumbled to Scott, but before he could respond there was a deafening and repetitive pounding on the windows. We all jumped and turned toward them only to see a massive onslaught of small black birds flying directly into the glass.

Karen and Dr. Arch gasped; the ghost hunter rushed toward the glass with his EMF device in hand and the historian from Harvard fainted.

A loud splintering sound echoed through the room as the ancient glass shattered against the assault. Then Cheryl called in a cheerful voice, "Cut!"

Two
······················

The fresh air buffeted my face as I followed Dr. Arch outside. The sky was dark, covered with a full black-bird migration, swarms of them passing the castle. On the grassy area in front of the castle were literally hundreds of dead blackbirds, as if they had been steamrolled by an imaginary vehicle. Behind me, Scott and Karen Kenley emerged from the castle, followed by several more cast, crew, and cameramen.

Scott laced his fingers through mine and pulled me back, away from the carnage. "Holy cow! This is terrible. I've never seen anything like it."

The cameramen began to shoulder their equipment and film the disaster. Out of the corner of my eye I could see Cheryl jumping up and down. This would be gold in her promo.

"What's going on?" Karen, the FBI profiler, asked.

"Blackbird migration," Scott said.

Growing up in the country, I knew that birds, or other animals, sensed things better than us humans. There was definitely something going on in our environment that was cause for alarm.

"This is a bad omen," Ashley, the paranormal docent, said.

The priest, Father Gabriel, agreed. "Yes, a bad omen. A sign of evil."

"That's ridiculous," Scott replied.

"It's not," Father Gabriel insisted.

The ghost hunter, Jack, laughed heartily. "Well, let's see if we can figure out what's happening here first."

Both men squared off against each other, glaring. I looked from one to the other, preparing to stop their quarrel.

Scott put a hand on my shoulder, stopping me from interfering. "Should we go back inside?" he asked. "They'll probably need help clearing the birds out of there."

I hated to leave, but followed him back into the castle anyway, which despite the awful squawking of the trapped birds, seemed quiet relative to the pandemonium outside. We climbed the rickety stairs together.

"What is it supposed to mean, do you think?" I asked Scott. "All those birds?"

"I don't know but it sure is creepy," he admitted.

"Definitely," I said.

We reached the second floor and darted past three birds that were flying down the hallway. Scott tore off his jacket and swatted at the birds matador-style to get them down the stairs and out the front door to freedom.

"I think we'll be clearing birds for days," I said.

No sooner were the words out of my mouth than another few birds flapped out of the library, one going for my dark hair as if I were a bush. I ducked, covering my head with my hands, as Scott batted it away from me. The other birds somehow found their way toward the open stairs and out of the castle.

"O . . . men," I said in an exaggerated way to Scott, who gave me his classic sideways grin.

"If the spirits don't get us, the birds will."

"Maybe Alfred Hitchcock is roaming these hallways," I joked.

Inside the library, the psychic, Bert, was still on his knees and the historian lady, Martha, was laid out flat on the floor. Only one crew member remained in the room and he was attending to Martha, fanning her and holding her wrist. Someone had propped a rolled-up jacket under her head.

"Anyone called 911?" Scott asked.

The crew member looked up. "Oh, that's not necessary. She'll come to in a minute," he said. "Her pulse is strong."

The psychic startled when he heard us. He grabbed my arm. "Georgia, I had a vision of you."

"Of me?" I asked. The hair on the back of my neck stood up and I pulled my arm out of his grip.

"Yes," he said dramatically. "You will have a visitor." His face was grim as he said it. Even though I really don't fancy myself a believer, goose bumps rose on my forearms.

"What kind of visitor?" Scott asked.

Before the psychic could reply, Cheryl bustled into the room.

"What a scene outside. I'm glad we've captured everything," she said, unable to contain the giddiness from her voice.

Scott laughed. "Yeah. It'll make a great promotion commercial. Right, Cheryl?"

"Absolutely," she said. "Oh!" She turned toward me. "I meant to tell you. Your father and Becca will be joining us for dinner tonight."

Relief flooded me. I looked at the psychic. "I guess that's my visitor," I said.

Cheryl and my father had been dating since they first met on the reality TV set of *Love or Money*, where my father had joined me for moral support. Right now, Dad was in the middle of his harvest season, so he'd stayed behind to work. Ordinarily, Scott and I would have helped him with the harvest, but because of the production timeline, my best friend, Becca, had agreed to help him in our stead.

"Who's Becca?" Bert asked.

"My assistant," Cheryl said. "Speaking of which"—she poked the crew member attending the historian on the shoulder—"what's going on here? Do we need a medic?"

He shook his head. "No, she's going to be fine. It's just

going to take a few minutes. I think I have some smelling salts in my kit. If you'll stay with her, maybe I can get them."

Cheryl waved a hand, dismissing him. He bolted out of the room, but before he could return, the historian's eyes fluttered open.

She struggled to raise her head.

I dropped to my knees and held her hand. "It's all right," I said. "You fainted. You'll feel better in a moment."

She blinked rapidly. "The birds, the awful pounding. It was terrible, wasn't it?" she asked.

"Yes," I said. The migration was largely over now, but the wind howled through the broken window drowning out my words.

The historian shivered.

I patted her arm. "You have some time to rest. We're done filming for the day and there's going to be a crew dinner tonight."

Cheryl nodded. "Cast and crew dinner in about an hour. You all can take a break. I'm going to find some crew to clean the birds out of the castle."

I helped Martha to her feet. Scott took one arm and I took the other, and together we walked her down the precarious steps.

Father Gabriel was on his way in from the outside. "Martha," he said. "Are you all right now, dear?"

"Yes," she greeted him. "I don't know what came over me. I found the whole thing rather frightful." He took her from us and escorted her outside.

"Some fresh air will do you good, darling," he said, as they walked out together.

Scott looked at me. "Well, I guess we got an hour to kill. What do you want to do? Walk around the castle?"

"Heck, no." I pushed the doors open to get us to the outside. "Let's stay outside for a while, let the crew get rid of the birds on the inside."

He laced his fingers through mine. "That sounds like a great idea."

We walked toward the dead birds that littered the garden area. "Predators will come tonight," I said.

He laughed. "Predators of all kinds."

"Yes," I agreed. "This show is going to take a toll on me."

"We have a good chance of winning, though," he said. "Think of that. Your dad can use the money to rebuild the farm and . . ." He hesitated.

"What is it?" I asked.

We'd been wanting to get the money so we could finally take our vacation together, hopefully get married, but since the accident, Scott hadn't talked much about our relationship.

He shrugged. "Nothing. I . . . Never mind."

Something about his demeanor bothered me. I knew it was tough on him after the mugging in Spain. He'd suffered a head injury and had even been in a coma for a week. Now at times, he couldn't seem to recall mundane things, but worse there seemed to be a strange vibe between us, something I couldn't quite put a finger on.

I suddenly felt the impulse to rush into his arms, so I

wrapped my arms around him and laid my head on his chest.

He sighed.

Sighing? Oh, that's bad!

Desperation flooded my heart. I wanted so much to turn the clock back, to go back to where we'd been before the accident. I squeezed his neck, moving my head from his chest and pressing my cheek against his, but he remained limp and listless in my arms.

Dread snaked its way through my belly.

Scott patted my back in an almost brotherly way that broke my heart, and stepped away.

Before I could ask him what was wrong, Dr. Arch approached us.

"Hey, you two lovebirds," he said. "Are you ready for the gala event?"

Scott smiled. "I don't think it's a *gala*. I think it's sandwiches and salad," he said.

My stomach rumbled. Despite sandwiches and salad being a far cry from what the senora had fixed us in Spain during our last show, I was still eager to eat. "There could be soup, if we're lucky. Shall we go help them set up?" I asked.

"Sounds like a plan," said Scott.

The tables in the dining room were set buffet-style. There were deli meats—roast beef, ham, turkey—all on one platter and different types of cheeses on another. Sliced bread and rolls of all kinds were in baskets nearby with small bowls of condiments next to them. Green, Greek, and macaroni salad made up the last of the offerings.

Scott stood next to me as he surveyed the sandwich fixings. "Not a bad spread," he said.

I nodded. I was hungry enough to be contented with cold cuts. "I don't think there are a lot of restaurants in Golden. Cheryl must have had a hard time organizing a catering service."

He nodded absently in agreement as we assembled our sandwiches.

I glanced toward the door to the dining room, eagerly awaiting my father and Becca. So far, they seemed to be at least an hour behind schedule.

Cheryl approached us.

"When are they getting here?" I asked.

She shrugged. "Gordon tried to call me a little earlier, but I missed his phone call," she said.

I reached into my back pocket to get my cell phone.

"Ah," Cheryl said, looking at me. "We'll need to take everyone's cell phone away tomorrow, so you better get whatever use out of it you can tonight."

"Why are you taking our cell phones?" I asked.

She wiggled her eyebrows at me. "Part of the game."

Scott glanced at me. "I have poor reception, in here anyway. You can have mine now." He took his phone out of his pocket and handed it to Cheryl.

She waved a hand at him. "No, no. We'll want to get you turning it in on camera."

Scott shrugged. "Have it your way."

"I'm having poor reception, too," Cheryl admitted. "Do you think it has to do with the energy in the castle?" she asked, looking around.

"You don't believe any of that stuff, do you?" I asked her.

"That it's haunted?" She glanced around nervously. "Well, the birds this afternoon were rather frightening, weren't they?"

"There is something going on," I said. "In the air, with the earth. They probably sensed something and wanted to do a mass migration out of the area. Believe me, I would join them if I could."

Cheryl shivered. "It's freezing in here. We're going to need to bring in some space heaters."

Several cast members behind me in the buffet line started to grumble. Cheryl waved at me, instructing me to finish loading up my plate, then scurried off. I took a piece of sliced provolone and put it on my sandwich and moved on. Scott followed suit.

We found a quiet corner to sit in, but before we could have any kind of discussion, the ghost hunter, Jack, and his partner, the psychic, Bert, joined us.

"Can we have a seat?" Bert asked.

Scott opened the palm of his hand, indicating the chair in front of us. "Be my guest," he said.

They sat across from us. "This place is great," Jack said. "I can't wait to have at it tomorrow with my instruments. Tonight, I've set up my EMF by the door. We should see if we have any paranormal activity by morning."

"Is Cheryl allowing that?" I asked.

He shrugged. "Why not? That's what we're here for. To discover what's going on with this castle, discover the story of Jane."

"I thought we were here to make a TV show," said Scott.

Bert laughed. "Well that, too, but if we can figure out who killed Jane, all the better," he said.

From the adjoining room came some noise that startled most of the cast and crew who were eating. We all looked up expectantly to see my father and Becca enter the room. I jumped up and ran toward them.

Dad was the first one to me, hugging me and lifting me into the air. "Georgia! How's it going? Have you already solved the mystery?" he asked.

I laughed, enjoying the closeness of my father and my best friend. "Not yet, but I certainly appreciate the vote of confidence."

Becca smiled. "Y'all have started filming, right? Bring us up to speed."

I led them over to the buffet table. Becca grabbed a paper plate and began piling sandwich fixings on it.

"Oh, there's plenty to tell," I said. I turned to my dad. "Did you see the blackbirds?"

He nodded. "Weather predictions say flooding in the area."

"Well, that explains it," I said.

California had suffered a drought for several years; now rain would pour in and flood the area. Mother Nature taking care of business.

Jack overheard us. "No, no. Unexpected blackbird migration is definite proof of paranormal activity," he said.

Becca looked at me, a smile playing on her lips. "That's what I heard."

I stifled a giggle.

She squeezed her way between Bert and Jack and placed her paper plate on the table. Bert seemed to perk up at her presence.

He offered a hand. "I'm Bert," he said happily. "Robert, but you can call me Bert. Everybody does."

She smiled. "I'm Rebecca, but you can call me Becca. Everybody does."

Bert beamed. "So much in common already."

Scott pinched my knee and we refrained from giggling.

Cheryl entered the room, followed by two crew members lugging some space heaters. She signaled to the far area for them to set them up, then joined us. She gave my father a chaste peck on the cheek. "Gordon, I'm glad you made it safely," she said.

He cleared a spot for her at our table and filled her water glass with a pitcher that was on it. Meanwhile, at the next table, I could overhear Father Gabriel chatting with his partner, Martha, who seemed fully recovered from her faint earlier in the day.

At their table were Ashley, the castle docent, and Jessica, the grand niece to Jane.

Father Gabriel said, "The castle should be cleared of evil spirits. I think tomorrow we should call on Saint Michael to help us."

"You don't really believe the place is haunted, do you?" Ashley asked.

Jessica quirked an eyebrow at her. "Well, don't you? I mean, you're the paranormal docent."

"Well, I believe," Ashley said, pressing a hand over her heart. "But so many people are skeptics."

Father Gabriel smiled at her. "I am not a skeptic, my dear. I am a man of faith."

Ashley's cheeks flushed red. "Right, right. Of course. I just . . . I mean, the blackbird stuff. That isn't proof of anything," she said.

At the next table, Dr. Arch sat with the FBI profiler, Karen Kenley. Their heads were huddled together in conversation. I wished I could overhear them.

I leaned close to Scott and jutted my chin toward Dr. Arch and Karen Kenley. "What do you think they're on about?"

He looked over at their table and shrugged. "I don't know, but I have to say I'd guess Dr. Arch is probably scheming something. He has that look about him."

Becca glanced over at their table. "Yeah, definitely. He's up to something. You can tell by his body language."

Bert twisted around in his seat to look at Dr. Arch.

"Any ideas, Bert? Are you a mind reader along with being psychic?" I teased.

He turned back around to face us. "No, no. Not a mind reader. But I am intuitive."

I smiled. "Intuitive, huh? That sounds like the sensitive type," I said, getting a kick out of how he colored.

Suddenly his chin dropped and I immediately regretted teasing him.

Had I embarrassed him?

Becca waved a hand. "Oh, don't listen to her. Georgia doesn't know anything about sensitivity. She's the furthest thing from it."

Now it was my turn to redden.

Three
....

Scott stiffened at Becca's comment, and patted my knee, but it somehow felt a bit insincere.

I stood. The entire table looked at me and I grew hot and uncomfortable. "I'm going to get some air."

Scott excused himself from the table and followed me. "Hey, wait up," he said. "I need to talk to you about something."

The serious expression on his face made my heart plummet into my stomach. I reached for his hand, only he wasn't expecting it and our hands bumped awkwardly. Ordinarily, Scott would have made a joke about it and wrapped his arms around me, but tonight we both dropped our arms to our respective sides and walked out of the room together in silence.

What was going on with him?

Outside of the main dining area, the castle was frigid. There were drafts running throughout every room and passageway; the broken window in the prayer room only made matters worse.

I shivered and said, "I think it's warmer outside than it is inside."

Scott shuffled his feet next to me. "Yeah. This time of year, it's like that in this area."

We walked outside. The grounds were enormous. We descended the back porch steps and went past the empty swimming pool onto the rolling grass. There was a large garden area surrounded by shrubbery and in the distance we could see planted vegetables, olive and grape groves, and wheat fields.

"The historical society's done a good job of keeping up the castle," I said. "At least the exterior."

"Yeah," Scott agreed. "The interior will never be the same. Looks like they knocked out the roof several years ago. That's the best way to destroy a building. The third and fourth floor are probably beyond repair," he said.

"That's sad," I said. The idea of something being beyond repair bothered me. I looked into Scott's dark eyes for comfort, but he averted his gaze.

"How'd you know about the roof?" I asked, trying to ignore the fact our conversation seemed clunky.

He shrugged. "Just a little online research I did earlier."

I nodded. The discomfort between us was palpable. Ordinarily, we'd be finishing each other's sentences and now there were large gaps of silence. A gust of wind blew around us, leaves rustling at our feet, my hair whipping at my face. This was the impending storm the blackbirds must have sensed.

"Are you feeling okay?" I asked Scott.

"Yeah." He shrugged. "Sure. Why not?"

"Well, it's just that you're very quiet," I said.

He shrugged again. "Aren't I normally quiet?"

"No," I said. "Not normally."

He got a distant look in his eye. "Not since the accident?" he asked.

I nodded sympathetically. "How do you feel about stuff in general?" I asked.

He looked at me. "What stuff in general?"

I meant me.

How do you feel about me? That's what I wanted to say, but I didn't have the courage to put my heart out on the line, so instead I shrugged and the futility of the gesture made my skin itch.

Suddenly, he grabbed my hand. "Georgia, I know we're in love . . ." His voice cracked with emotion and he swallowed. "But I have a . . ." He sighed. "I have a problem. I'm not *feeling* in love. I don't know how to explain it, and I don't want you to take it the wrong way. I'm so sorry."

Fear wrapped around my heart and my breath caught.

What was he saying?

Was he breaking up with me?

Oh, God. After everything we'd been through, he was going to break up with me.

He squeezed my hand harder. "I don't know what to say. I just need you to be patient with me. I . . . Like I said, my brain knows that we were in love. I'm just trying to tell my heart that."

"You don't *feel* like you're in love with me?" I asked. The question sputtered out of my lips. I hadn't wanted to say it, hadn't wanted to confirm what he was telling me. Now I wished I could stuff the words back into my mouth.

He nodded. "I . . . I like you a lot," he said. "I know that. You're funny and you're smart, and you're beautiful. I know you're going to figure out this mystery, and win the contest and all that. I just . . . I'm just trying to keep up with stuff," he admitted.

My chest suddenly hollowed out and tears burned at my eyes.

He doesn't love me?

My heart ached so much, it was difficult to breath.

Scott's head hung down and for a moment he looked so lost, I thought I'd weep. I wrapped my arms around him and said with more desperation in my voice than I'd planned, "Scott! Scott! Everything's going to be fine."

Part of me wanted to tell him, "You'll remember being in love with me! You'll fall in love with me again, won't you?" But I couldn't say it.

Tears streamed down my cheeks.

"What do you want to do?" I asked.

He wiped my tears, his warm hands on my face only making me feel more desperate.

"Just give me time," Scott said. "Just give me a little bit of time."

Another burst of wind tore at us, howling and whipping around us, almost separating us with its icy bluster.

"I want you to know, if I'm different, I don't mean to be," he continued. "I'm just being the only way I know how to be right now . . . I'm trying to remember things."

I nodded, pulling away from him. I rubbed at my eyes and face, and tried to keep my head from exploding. This had come as such a surprise. I'd known things were awkward between us, but I never suspected he didn't love me anymore.

Before Scott, I'd been left at the altar and now all the feelings of betrayal came rushing back at me, hitting me squarely in the solar plexus. I sucked air in greedily, hoping it would calm my racing heart.

"Not remember things exactly," Scott said, barely noticing that I was practically hyperventilating. "That's not the right word. I remember things, but it's as if those memories belong to someone else. As if I'm not invested in them somehow."

He's been in a severe accident, I reminded myself.

He'd been in a coma. Head injuries take a lot of healing time. We'd been so lucky he'd mostly recovered quickly. The doctors had all said it might take time for life to return to normal. I just hadn't thought that that diagnosis had included our relationship.

There was life before the accident and life after the accident.

"I'm like Humpty Dumpty," he said.

"No," I said. "Not Humpty Dumpty."

"Yes," he said. "They couldn't put him back together again."

Before I could argue, footsteps sounded behind us. I turned to look, but no one was there.

"Did you hear that?" I asked him.

He shrugged. "Hear what? Are you listening to what I'm telling you?"

"Yes! Yes!" I grabbed his hands. "Of course, I'm listening," I said. "You're . . ." And then my mind went blank. I'd been about to say, "You're breaking up with me," but he wasn't really, was he? He was only asking for a little bit of time. He was asking to have some space to figure things out.

I could give him space. I could do that.

"I can give you space," I said, offering him my most reassuring smile.

Disappointment flashed through his eyes, then he narrowed them at me. "Right. Yeah. Space."

"Space," I said. "Isn't that what you asked for? Space?"

"I asked you to be patient," he said.

"Yes. That's what I meant. Patient. I won't rush things. I . . ." I stuttered and looked at the ground. Nothing I was going to say in this moment would make anything right. All I could do was be patient. I grabbed for his hands, but they remained at his sides, so I dropped mine awkwardly. "I love you, Scott, and I remember everything and I can feel the love for the both of us. I can love you enough for the both of us."

He stepped away from me. "No, Georgia, you can't. Don't you get it? That's what I'm saying! You can't love me enough to make me *feel* in love. It just doesn't work that way."

"What?" I asked. Panic clawed at my throat. The conversation was going all wrong. I wanted to say something to make it better, but I was speechless.

"Never mind," he said. Annoyance flashed across his face, his jaw tightening. "Nothing's right, right now. It's me. It's not you," he said. "Okay? It's me. I'm so sorry." His dark eyes turned stormy with sorrow and my heart broke even further. Then, he turned on a heel and walked away from me.

I made to follow him, to call out to him, and then I remembered I wasn't supposed to follow. I was supposed to give him space or be patient or whatever it was that two people who were in love did when things weren't going right.

My eyes burned and I wanted desperately to sit down and have an ugly cry. I glanced around the garden, searching out a space. There was a stone bench near some rosebushes that looked like the right kind of spot to have my meltdown. I swallowed back the lump in my throat and crossed the garden.

Some defensive part of my brain scanned the shrubbery for interlopers. It would be just like Cheryl to send a cameraman out here to film my demise.

Ugh. The show.

Scott and I were supposed to be partners on the show for the next few weeks, and now what?

We were supposed to pretend everything was fine between us? Act like a couple or just good friends?

My head ached just thinking about it and a sob escaped my lips. Just as I was about to reach the solace of the stone bench, footsteps sounded again behind me.

I whirled around to look. I was sure there was somebody out there, but only the empty garden lay in front of me.

The hair on my neck rose.

I was alone here in the garden, wasn't I?

Or did I have company? Either the human or paranormal kind . . . ?

No, that was ridiculous. I was letting the spooky mansion get to me.

Rustling sounds came from the bushes.

It could be the wind . . .

I cautiously followed the sound, stepping silently toward it. In the distance, I could hear a pair of voices arguing. What was going on? Somebody was having a fight. I tried to follow the sound, but hedges divided us.

I circumnavigated the hedges, walking back to where the swimming pool lay. I passed the decaying empty swimming pool and headed toward the voices.

Then suddenly, Dr. Arch appeared from behind a hydrangea bush.

I leapt back and covered my heart with my hand.

"Georgia. I'm sorry. Did I alarm you?"

"No, no," I lied. The stubborn ex-cop part of me would never admit to being alarmed or caught off guard.

"What are you doing out here? Taking a little walk?" he asked.

I took a step back. "I could ask you the same. What are you doing out here?"

He smiled broadly, baring his overly whitened, large teeth at me. "I'm having a little walk myself. Getting some fresh air, exploring the castle and the grounds. I assume you're doing the same?"

His question hung in the air, giving me the creeps. How long had he been out here? Had he been following Scott and me? Had he been listening to our conversation?

I turned away from him. "Um, yes. Although I think I've had enough air for one night."

Four
....

I stormed away from Dr. Arch and headed back toward the pool area. I walked around the cracked concrete, imagining the pool and the castle in their heyday. It had been created in the Victorian era with medallions and wainscoting and all sorts of chandeliers that must have made it charming in its time. It was difficult to imagine it as a reform school. It seemed more like the sort of place that would have housed a royal family.

Although, I knew full well the juvenile delinquents had been relegated to the basement. These same delinquents would have been sent to San Quentin before the castle was built. And then during the Depression, families had dropped off children here they couldn't provide for.

The reform school had been run military-style. The program had been very successful, with an extremely low recidivism rate. The young adults had been given skills of tailoring and woodworking and they'd learned farming.

I admired the view of the rolling acres. This fertile land had been able to provide for the hundreds of people living in the castle and the outlying buildings that surrounded it. Still today, there were small outbuildings where some of the historical society's current staff lived.

The historical society's main mission was to renovate the castle and its grounds. Restore its former glory. I imagined the pool renovated and filled with clean water.

A romantic vision of Scott and me sitting poolside, sipping margaritas, sprang into my mind, only to be accompanied by a hollowness in my belly. What if what Scott and I had . . . had been lost forever? Our loving relationship left to die and decay, like the castle.

Could there be a restoration for us?

As I stood there lost in thought, the sound of gravel crunching underfoot startled me. I whirled around to see Becca approach.

She wiggled her fingers at me. "Hey, you."

When I nodded without speaking, she asked, "What's going on? We haven't even had a chance to talk."

"Yeah," I offered halfheartedly.

A frown creased her delicate skin as she evaluated my mood. I knew she could tell something was wrong, but apparently she'd decided to try to sidestep the issue by asking, "What's up with Bert? Do you know anything about him? He's so cute."

"Sure," I said. "If you like lumberjack psychics."

She giggled nervously. "Yeah. He's hot."

"If you like hair," I countered.

She laughed. "Well, obviously, you don't." Being that Scott was bald, it was fair of her to say that. But instead of laughing, I looked at the ground, fighting the feeling of misery that threatened to envelop me.

"Hey," she said, closing the distance between us, until her face was right up to mine. "What's wrong? I'm sorry about the sensitivity crack—"

"It's not that," I said. I relayed to her what Scott had said.

She put her arm around me. "Oh, honey. Don't listen to him. He's just being a guy. They're commitment-phobes. You know that from Paul. Scott will be himself in no time," she said.

Paul was my former fiancé, the one who had stranded me at the altar. After having been burned so awfully in front of family and friends, I'd been hoping my relationship with Scott would have a better, more happily-ever-after type of ending.

I shrugged. "It's all different this time. Scott is different."

I hated to admit it, but after being in a coma, after his head injury in Spain, he was different. Did I still love him? I searched my heart. Undoubtedly, I did, but was I in love with who I knew Scott had been? Was I being realistic about who he was now?

Becca poked me. "Hey, don't go there."

"Go where?" I asked.

"In your head. I know where you're going, off to some dark place."

I looked at her, my mouth agape. "How do you know?"

"Because I've known you for a long time, silly," she said. "You're wondering if you even love him, and you do, okay?"

I shrugged. "Okay."

"So, tell me about the cast," she said.

She was changing the subject to prevent me from going off the deep end of dismal. I took the bait. "What can I tell you? They're crazy."

"Well, not any more so than you." She laughed.

I shrugged. "Probably."

"Cheryl did a good job casting. I think Dr. Arch and Karen are going to be your most formidable competition," she said.

"Dr. Arch is creepy." I told her about him sneaking up behind me earlier.

She quirked an eyebrow. "I saw him leave the dining room after you and Scott. I didn't really think anything about it, but maybe he thought you guys were out to investigate a little, or explore something. You know there are parts of the castle off limits, right?"

"Everywhere's off limits, unless Cheryl gives us an explicit okay." I stood with my feet shoulder-width apart and placed one fist on my hip and the other hand midair with a stern finger pointed outward, in a mock imitation of Cheryl's stance when she lectured us.

Becca laughed. She knew Cheryl's lectures better than I did.

"So, you think Arch followed us?"

Becca frowned. "I don't know. He's kind of a strange cat. It's hard to get a read on him."

"Well, he's from L.A.," I said. "What do you expect?"

Becca smiled. "Yeah, everyone in L.A. is pretty strange, aren't they? Well, maybe not L.A., but Hollywood, definitely."

Together we crossed the pool area, the gravel path turned to sand, and we took a seat near some potted plants that overlooked more of the castle's acreage. "Are you going back to Dad's farm soon?" I asked.

"Yes. Your Dad has a nice harvest coming in. I asked Cheryl if she'll let me have a little bit more time off and . . . you know she'd do anything to help Gordon out. So he and I are planning on driving back tonight."

"Get to work in the morning bright and early that way," I finished for her.

She nodded. "Exactly."

"I wish Scott and I could go, too . . ."

We shared an awkward silence. I wanted to rewind my life. Go back to the simplicity of farm life. Feel the gratification of a great almond harvest, but mostly just to feel secure with where Scott and I stood.

After a moment, Becca asked, "Do you want me to talk to him?"

She meant Scott. I knew what she meant and I wanted to tell her no, but instead I asked, "What would you say?"

She shrugged. "I can offer to show him clips of himself on *Love or Money*. Show him how over-the-moon in love he was with you."

I laughed. "That's not a bad idea."

"It'll come back to him. I promise," she said.

"I hope you're right."

She squeezed my elbow. "I have news for you."

I raised an eyebrow at her. "Good news, I hope."

"Well, I got a message from the *Globe Tracker* show."

"What?" I asked.

"You know the show. They explore different phenomenas around the world. They usually have a cast of experts trying to explain away the weird stuff they see."

I nodded. "Yeah. It's one of my favorite shows. I loved the Stonehenge special."

Becca smiled. "I know. Well, they have an opening for a subject matter expert."

I stared at her. "What does that mean? What are you saying?"

"I think they want to make you an offer to be on their show. To go on various different episodes and be, you know, a talking head."

Her message took me by surprise. I had no career plans for after this show, and now another show was making me a full-time offer?

"I don't know, Becca. I don't know what to say."

She laughed. "Well, it is contingent on one thing."

"What's that?" I asked.

"You have to do well on *Cold Case in the Castle*. You have to stay to the end. Or at least be in the final four. They want someone with a significant following, and since this show is based on viewer votes, they think if you have enough of an audience to keep you on, then you'd be a good bet for their show. They think you could bring your audience to that show."

I dug the toe of my boot into the sand. "I don't know." I sighed. "Now with Scott feeling the way he does . . ."

"No. You can't back out of the show," she said. "You have to do well. Get to the final four. Then we can arrange something for the *Globe Tracker* show. If not, they'll probably go for someone else on this show that does well."

"Like Dr. Arch?" I asked.

"Maybe. Or maybe the paranormal docent." She wrinkled her nose.

"Yeah, that girl is a little strange, isn't she?" I asked.

Becca gave me a half shrug.

"What is it about her?" I probed.

Becca rolled her shoulders and said, "You know I can't tell you everything. At least, not stuff about the show."

So the docent had a secret that Cheryl was protecting. Becca would protect it, too, especially if it meant keeping her job.

Night was falling and it was beginning to get dark. Becca said, "Well, I guess you better get inside."

"Are you heading out?" I asked.

"Yeah, in a little bit," she said. "The crew is spending

the night over at the Indian casino and resort. Cheryl might be able to convince Gordon to try his hand at the craps table."

"There's no way she'll get Dad to go," I said. There was a casino a few miles up the road. Dad was completely opposed to gambling as his grandfather had lost his entire estate playing poker in casinos in Montana back in the day. His own father moved from Montana to California and had to start from scratch with nothing. Unfortunately, he'd been a gambler, too, and dad had inherited the gambling debts.

Dad had made a solemn oath never to set foot in a casino, and to my knowledge he never had.

Becca nodded. She knew my father almost as well as I did. "I know. I told Cheryl she's crazy. Anyway, be prepared for a rough ride tomorrow. Likely the crew will be partying all night. They're going to be cranky in the morning when they have to leave the room service behind."

"Where do we spend the night?" I asked.

She pointed back to the castle.

A chill overcame me. "In there?"

Becca giggled.

"Are there bedrooms?" I asked.

"Yes, but you won't get one."

Things had just gone from bad to worse. Then a large raindrop hit me in the face. When I looked up storm clouds rumbled by, opening into a light drizzle.

Becca felt the mist, too, and folded her arms across

her chest. "The crew's rolling out some sleeping bags for everyone in the main living room," she said. "You know, the historical society normally does overnight paranormal tours. So motion-sensor cameras are already set up. Cheryl loves that. Anyway, the cameras will catch any shenanigans; either drama going on with the cast or paranormal activity."

"You're kidding?" I asked.

The light drizzle was quickly turning into a shower. Becca covered her head and flashed me a wicked smile. "Of course not."

"It's freezing in there! And dark!"

"The cameras have night vision, but maybe I can talk Cheryl into giving you all some candles?"

"Don't. The paranormal kooks in there will want to hold a séance."

Becca giggled and gave me a farewell hug. "Oh, you know you're a kook at heart."

nside, the crew had completed the makeover of the main living area: The sleeping bags lined the floor. I spotted Scott's long, lean body resting on top of one of the bags in the corner, his legs crossed, his boots still on. I had the mad desire to rush in and cuddle him, but instead I walked up to him awkwardly and stood in front of him in silence.

"Hey," he said, smiling up at me. He patted the sleeping bag next to him. "Take a load off."

"Is that okay?" I asked.

"Come on. Don't be like that," he said. "I was just trying to be honest with you."

I stepped over him and onto the sleeping bag he'd left for me. "I know. I want to respect what you said."

He put his arms around me. "Okay, well then just don't be weird about it."

How was I not supposed to be weird about the fact that he told me he didn't feel like he was in love with me anymore?

"I won't be," I said, making a mental note to try to act normal around him.

The paranormal docent, Ashley, and her partner, Jessica, came over to us. Ashley hightailed it into the far sleeping bag, leaving the one next to me empty.

I indicated the sleeping bag and said to Jessica, "Make yourself comfy."

She climbed in next to me. "Oh, good. This place creeps me out. I'll feel better lying here between you and Ashley."

Bert and Jack came into the room next and took a pair of sleeping bags across from us. Father Gabriel was pacing the room, but his partner, Martha, was already fast asleep in a sleeping bag near Bert and Jack. In the far corner were Dr. Arch and Karen Kenley. Their heads were together, and they appeared to be frantically plotting something.

"What do you think the doctor's up to?" Jessica asked.

"I was wondering the same thing myself," I said.

Ashley wiggled her eyes at us. "Maybe we need a spy."

"Sure," I said and tapped Jack's foot. "Go make nice to Karen. See what she tells you about the doctor."

Jack snorted, "Yeah. I already tried to make nice to her. She ignored me. Flapped her black hair right in my face."

Jessica laughed. "I'm sure it wasn't personal."

He grunted at her. "I'm sure it was. Anyway, I'm going to put up my electromagnetic field instrument in the corner and see what information I can get."

It was my turn to snort. "It's rainy now and it's an electrical storm. Won't that mess up your readings?" I asked.

As if in answer, Mother Nature let loose with a large rumble followed by a flash of light.

Jack jumped excitedly, examining his device. "Look at that! I've never seen it light up like that before."

"It's the storm," I said, but he ignored me as he rushed to another corner of the room, chasing the little beeps coming from his instrument.

Bert sat up, resting the palms of his hands on the floor, and leaning back into them. He stared at me. "Tell me more about your friend."

"Well, you're a psychic. You should know everything already," I answered.

Scott poked me. "Don't be mean."

"Was I being mean?" I asked.

"Becca's great," Scott said, "A very nice girl. You two could be good together if you treat her well."

Bert nodded, silently taking some hint from Scott that I hadn't caught.

The light in the room was fading as the night grew longer. "I don't think I'm going to be able to sleep in here," Jessica said. "It's so dark."

The darker the room grew, the louder the rain seemed to hammer.

"Does anybody have a flashlight?" I asked.

"You have one on your phone, don't you?" Scott asked.

I pulled out my phone, disappointed to find the low-battery icon flashing, for a few moments, anyway. It was surprising how dark it was inside the room. A nervous energy ran through me.

Wings fluttered down the corridor, and Martha, who I thought had been sound asleep, shrieked, "The birds!"

Inside the room, someone rustled over to her, then Father Gabriel's voice soothed. "Now, Martha, don't worry. Even if some are still trapped in the castle, the doors to this room are closed. They won't get in here."

"Which is a good thing," Dr. Arch said. "There's probably a colony of bats in the rafters."

Something scurried across the floor near our heads.

Next to me, Jessica sprang up. "What was that?"

"Probably a field mouse," I said.

"Ewww!" Jessica said, shuddering. "Please tell me you're joking."

On the other side of me, Scott chuckled.

I patted Jessica's arm. "We're in the middle of the

country. This castle has more leaks and drafts than my Dad's old barn. What do you think it was?"

She gripped my hand. "OMG! I'm not going to be able to sleep with rats running around."

"Not a rat," I said. Even though in all likelihood it could have been rat. "A little field mouse. A harmless little guy, like Mickey Mouse."

"Think of it as a hamster," Ashley cooed.

"As long as you washed your face, you'll be all right," Scott offered.

Jessica stiffened. "What's that got to with anything?"

Jack chimed in. "Well, hopefully you didn't put on any night cream, right?"

Jessica let out a little squeal of alarm. "Why?"

"They like the smell. They think it's food and they're liable to come over and lick your face," Bert said.

Jessica was up like rocket. She shot toward the hallway door, screaming and picking up her feet like she was trying to outrun Michael Flatley. She reached the door in record time and gripped the handle, then let out another shriek. "It's locked! They locked us in here."

From outside, a howling sound reverberated and filled the room. Then came the unmistakable growling and snarling of animals fighting.

"The predators found the blackbirds," Scott whispered.

"Yup," I said. "It's going to be a long night."

Five
·················

slept poorly that night. Not because of the storm, or any paranormal activity I feared was afoot in the castle, nor even the close sleeping quarters of the cast. It was the conversation between Scott and me that weighed heavily on my heart.

When morning came, the cast arose rowdily. I think everyone was basically overjoyed that we'd been let loose from our cramped, rodent-infested quarters.

We were given a continental breakfast in the dining room. Bagels, cream cheese, and some fruit were laid out for us. As we piled food on our plates, I realized that my father had left the evening before, and I hadn't even had a chance to say good-bye.

I must have sighed out loud, because Scott nuzzled his chin into my shoulder and whispered, "What?"

The sudden closeness to him made my heart race. "What?" I repeated. I was so keenly aware of how his feelings were lagging behind mine that it made me feel on guard.

"You sighed," he said.

"Ah," I said. "I didn't get a chance to see my dad before he left, and I was just missing him."

Scott nodded his understanding, but before he could respond, Cheryl blustered into the room. "All right, everyone, make sure to have a hearty breakfast. We'll be filming all day and I want everyone to look alive." She giggled. "Well, I want *you all* to look alive." She glanced at the walls of the castle. "Any of you undead specters that want to make an appearance today, don't feel pressure about your looks, we'll take you the way you are."

Father Gabriel stiffened. "This is no laughing matter. If a spirit is stuck here on this plane, I'm more than happy to attempt to clear it."

Cheryl held up a hand. "Oh, no you don't, father. We've had this conversation. If you clear the spirits, I don't have a show."

"Plus, honestly, the historical society wouldn't like it, either," Ashley said.

Father Gabriel made a face. "Child, we can't be selfish like that. We must—"

"Never mind about that right now," Cheryl interrupted. "After breakfast, I want you all to get into hair and makeup, and then meet again in the prayer room after that."

Martha stiffened. "The prayer room? With the broken window?"

Cheryl smiled. "Precisely! We'll pick up where we left off yesterday."

Ashley was standing next to me in the buffet line. I turned to her and asked, "Why would the historical society care if Father Gabriel cleared the spirits?"

She smoothed cream cheese onto half a garlic bagel. "Oh! That's how they make most of their money for the renovation and stuff. The paranormal overnights, the masquerade balls, and Hollywood shows like ours that want to film here and all that. If the castle wasn't haunted, they'd be out of business. Do you know what this place rakes in on Halloween alone?"

"Specters are spectacular for the pocketbook," Jack said, chomping into a bagel. "Just look at Hearst Castle."

Ashley agreed. "Yeah! That's the goal. Some of the staff here want Golden Castle to grow as big as Hearst, but the renovation has to be funded before that can become a reality."

After breakfast, the cast split up. The men were to go to one area for their touch-ups, while the women were to go to a separate area. I was lucky enough to get my own makeup chair in a small private room off to the side of the main hallway.

Kyle, as usual, was my makeup artist. We'd been together for three shows now and I knew how temperamental he could get. Still, I was happy to have him. Better the devil you know.

He was dressed in his usual flashy style with burgundy pants and a short black bolero jacket.

"You look nice," I said.

He ran a hand through his sandy blond hair and spun around for me. "Oh, you like? I got the jacket and pants when we were in Spain. Shoes, too. Aren't they something? They feel like slippers."

The shoes were caramel-colored leather with dark brown strips crisscrossing the toes and arch area. They were undoubtedly the most gorgeous pair of shoes I'd seen in a long time.

"Handcrafted," Kyle continued, when he caught me admiring his footwear.

"I wish I'd had a chance to go shopping while we were in Spain," I said, with more than a little jealousy floating in my voice.

"Well, sister, it wasn't cheap. Let me tell you. It's a good thing I won five hundred bucks at the Indian casino last night or I wouldn't be able to pay my credit card bill this month." He sat me down in the makeup chair and asked, "What happened to you? Didn't you sleep well? You've got bags so large under your eyes it's a crime you don't have a plane ticket to go with 'em."

I rubbed at my eyes and groaned. "I do?"

He nodded and unzipped a large duffel bag of makeup.

I shrugged. Even though Kyle and I could be chatty, I wasn't about to go into the details of my love life with him. Nevertheless, he said, "I hope you're not having trouble with the hunk."

"That's none of your business," I said.

He grunted and pulled out a pot of foundation. He got to work on my face, saying, "Well, if I have to use up all my concealer on you, it is my business."

"Let's just say, it's hard to get a good night's sleep with bats and rats running around—"

Kyle let out a scream and bit his knuckle.

I laughed. "It wasn't that bad."

"And I thought we had it rough at the casino. There was absolutely nothing good on my pay-per-view and my pillow was hard as a rock." He applied color to my cheeks and then got to work on my eyes. "I'm going for a more casual look here than glam, glam, because of our setting. But I hope you'll still be pleased."

"I'm sure I will," I soothed.

In reality, I would have been happy to run around in sweatpants and work boots all day, but I knew Cheryl wanted everyone to look "Hollywood casual," which meant you had to put in more work to try to look natural than you did to look glamorous. It made no sense.

When Kyle was done with my hair and makeup, I climbed up the first-floor stairs to the prayer room.

Most of the cast were already present, but Scott and Jessica were still missing. Harris, our fearless host, was standing at a podium in front of some of the cast.

A morning breeze blew through the broken window, and I peered outside. After last night's feeding frenzy, all that remained of the blackbirds that had perished yesterday were clumps of feathers. Still, the air was fresh with a clean smell that only comes after a good rain.

I took my spot next to Dr. Arch, who turned on his heel to appraise me. "Georgia, don't you look beautiful." He smiled and the sight of his large teeth reminded me again that there were predators all around me.

I wanted to ignore him, but he wasn't a man to take lightly.

He leaned closer to me. "Is everything all right?"

"Fine," I said. "Just focusing on what I need to do to solve the mystery." I eyed him. He and Karen Kenley likely had the best chance of winning. Had he already been offered a spot on *Globe Tracker*?

Before long, the rest of the cast showed up. Scott and Jessica walked in together. He took his place next to me, and squeezed my hand. He gave me his winning smile, and for a moment my heart soared. He winked at me, and then I realized he was sending me a message. We were supposed to look happy on camera, not let on that we were having any trouble. Even though my heart seemed to bottom out from under me, I nodded and gave his hand a reassuring squeeze.

Cheryl entered the room. She clapped her hands and got our attention. "All right, everybody," she said. "Time to take your places. Harris is going to instruct you to hand in any equipment you brought with you, cell phones, laptops, any of that paranormal paraphernalia." She waved her hand in a dismissive fashion.

"What?" the ghost hunter asked. "What do you mean?" He clutched his paranormal tool to his chest.

"Just that, what I said," she answered.

"But how are we supposed to measure all the activity in the castle?" Jack protested. "And there's tons, let me tell you!"

"Hand in our phones? What if we need the tools on them?" Martha complained. Then her face paled and she said, "Or worse! What if we have to call for help?"

Cheryl waved her hand again, ignoring all the grumbling. "Don't worry. You're not being cut off from civilization, for crying out loud. My crew has phones." Martha didn't seem soothed by the idea. In fact, she looked ready to complain further. But Cheryl cut her off by barking, "Places. Places, everyone." She put on a headset and retreated to the back of the room.

Harris came to life in front of the camera, booming in his made-for-TV voice. "Hello, America! And welcome back to *Cold Case in the Castle*!" He launched into a brief introduction of the cast, to remind the viewing audience about us. I imagined they'd edit in our names and roles in a neatly printed banner underneath our faces.

The cameras all panned us and we pasted smiles across our faces when we saw the small red light homed in on us.

Harris clapped his hands together. "All right, everyone. As you may know, we're eager to get on to solving the mystery of the murder of Jane Reiner. However, in order to do that, we need everybody on equal footing. Therefore, we're going to ask everyone to turn in any phones, laptops, or any other equipment you've brought with you."

The cast grumbled as we put our phones into a basket that was passed around. Harris looked satisfied, an evil grin on his face. "But we understand, in a high-tech world everyone needs a little help getting started with their mystery solving, so we've thought ahead for you. Throughout the castle is hidden: a laptop, a battery, a power charger, a network card, and some additional equipment that you all might find handy in solving the mystery."

The cast made some rumblings, but before anyone could protest too verbosely, Harris pulled out a box. "Now we're going to have ourselves a good old-fashioned scavenger hunt. As you get to know the castle, so will our viewer. Inside this box is a clue to where one of the items is located. In order to be fair, we've mixed it up, so everyone will have a chance to pull at random."

He called out, "Jessica!"

Jessica approached him. He held the box toward her. "Well, Jessica, let's go ahead and try your luck."

Jessica stuck her hand into the box and pulled out a slim piece of paper.

"Go ahead, read it," Harris encouraged.

She unfolded the paper and looked at the print. "Argh, matey. Any good captain would never be caught dead without one." She frowned and looked at Harris.

He shrugged. "Up to you, my dear."

She returned to the lineup.

Next up, Harris called Father Gabriel. He approached

and picked a note card out of the box. Harris nodded, and Father Gabriel unfolded the paper.

"Come here if you want to be closer to God," he read. He smiled. "Well, I assume this means my clue is in the chapel, although everyone should know God can be found everywhere."

Harris gave Father Gabriel a tight smile. Next up was Karen Kenley, the FBI profiler.

She picked out her slip of paper and read, "If I were a book, this would be my favorite place." She smiled and tapped the paper. "I think I know where to go."

After several more, it was finally my turn. When I approached, my clue read, "On a hot day, I love to take a dip here."

Harris smiled at me.

I retreated back to the cast line.

The pool.

Scott gave me a grin, and for a moment I suddenly felt that all was right with us.

As soon as Harris gave us the go-ahead, the cast scattered in different directions, a cameraman following each of us. I left the castle with my cameraman in tow. His name was Adam and although we didn't know each other well, he seemed friendly enough. He had a full beard and clear sharp eyes that gave me the impression he didn't miss much. Together we headed out toward the back, toward the pool. He had me stop a few times and refilm the exit of the building.

"Don't we need to get on with this?" I asked, impatiently

jamming my foot against the rotting floorboard on the porch.

He shrugged. "Go inside and exit the castle again. The light's not right."

"The others are going to find their clues, their equipment, and get started before I even have a chance to get to the pool," I complained.

He laughed. "Don't worry. It's all a big setup."

"What do you mean?" I asked.

He gave me a crooked grin. "You know I'm not supposed to say."

"Say it anyway," I said.

"Well, you know how Cheryl is." He adjusted the camera on his shoulder, and I realized he was turning it off so our conversation wouldn't be recorded. "Everybody will find something, but it's pretty useless."

"What do you mean?" I said.

He chuckled. "She wants you all to work together. It makes for better TV. You know, make alliances with some, make outcasts of others, that kind of thing."

"Oh, brother," I said. I'd known there'd be a catch. What, I wasn't exactly sure, but it'd be forthcoming.

He hoisted the camera back onto his shoulder and began to film me again. I entered the castle and this time when I exited, he didn't stop me, so I said, "Come on, then. Let's get over to the pool."

As we walked toward the pool, he said, "Wait up. Wait up. I want to get you next to these roses."

Surrounding the perimeter of the pool were beautiful

roses in full bloom. I let him capture me walking beside the rosebushes.

"Do you want me to pick one and smell it or anything corny like that?" I asked.

"No. No, this is fine. Just try to look like you're enjoying yourself," he said.

Guilt plagued me.

"Don't I look like I'm enjoying myself?"

"You really have to ask?" he said.

I knew he was right. I was probably scowling. A large part of me couldn't stand all the Hollywood hype, but I wanted to know what had happened to poor Jane. I wanted to find justice for her, and if playing along for the cameras was part of getting to the bottom of the case, I'd do it.

I pasted a smile on my face and did the best I could, all the while fighting the desire to dash toward the pool. Finally, when he waved at me that he'd gotten enough footage, I beelined toward the pool. It was empty and dilapidated, the bottom of it peeling, but that's not what bothered me. A lump was visible almost as soon as I turned the corner.

I gasped, my blood pressure skyrocketing, and I raced toward the ladder of the pool.

The cameraman said, "What the—"

"There's someone down there," I said.

I scurried over to the railing and climbed down into the pool.

The cameraman rushed over, close behind me. "Wait, wait! Maybe you shouldn't go down there."

But I couldn't stop myself.

Oh, my goodness.

It was a body.

Six

....

reached the last rung of the ladder and jumped to the floor of the pool. My heart racing, I prayed, "Oh, Lord. Please don't let him be dead."

But as I got closer, my gut screamed at me that it was a false hope. The man was unmoving and crumpled at such an odd angle that it didn't seem there was any way possible he was still alive. Against my better judgment, I flipped him over and evaluated him.

The man seemed to be in his late sixties, with a scruffy white beard and gray hair. His eyes were screwed shut, but his mouth was open and his expression was anxious. There was a large gash over his left eye, but not much blood.

I took his pulse. None. The cameraman, Adam, had his lens trained on me.

"Call 911," I yelled up at him.

He hesitated to put the camera down.

"Call 911," I shouted again, this time anger flaring up inside me. Was nothing sacred to these people? They cared only about capturing the moment on camera, no respect for this poor man's dignity.

Adam grunted and pulled his cell phone out of his pocket. He dialed rapidly. "Uh . . ." he stammered. "We need an ambulance."

"Not an ambulance," I called to him.

He went a little pale and asked, "He's dead?"

I sighed. "Well, he's not sipping margaritas down here."

"What do you want me to tell them?" he asked, referring to the 911 operator.

"Tell them we found a body and to send a black-and-white." While he mumbled a few things into the phone, I examined the scene around me.

There was a black sack in the corner of the pool. That was probably the package intended for me to find. I ignored it and glanced around for other clues.

What could have happened? Had he fallen into the pool overnight?

Last night, there'd been a lot of predators roaming around. Could he have been spooked by a bobcat or a coyote? Maybe he lost his footing and fell into the empty pool.

I regretted turning him over now. I'd disrupted his position and that was sure to rattle the investigating officer. I closed my eyes and imagined the body before I'd flipped him over. His arms hadn't been flayed out, the way one would expect if he'd been trying to break his fall.

What had happened, then?

The cameraman called down to me. "Georgia, they said someone's on their way." He shuffled his feet in the dirt and grimaced. "Man, Cheryl is going to freak out about this."

I reached the ladder and climbed up out of the pool. "Yeah. I think we'll have to tell her to halt production."

A look of fear crossed Adam's face. "Halt production?"

"We just found a body! We can't keep filming as if nothing happened," I said.

Adam pressed his lips together nodding, then said, "She's going to hate that."

"Right," I said. "She'll want to use this unfortunate incident somehow to leverage the show, get publicity."

"You know it," he said, handing his phone to me.

"What?"

"You call her. She'll take it better coming from you."

Despite the situation, I laughed. Cheryl wouldn't take it any better coming from me, but at least I knew she wouldn't fire me. I took his phone and dialed her number.

"What's going on, Adam?" she barked into the phone.

"It's me, Georgia," I said.

She let out a groan. "This can't be good." Suddenly, she appeared on the balcony from the second floor. "What's going on down there?" she called.

I disconnected the call. "We found a body," I shouted up to her.

"What?" she said. "Who?"

"I don't know. I don't recognize him," I told her.

"I swear, you're bad luck!" She pointed an accusing finger at me. "Not a word to anyone else. You understand? I'll be right down."

Begrudgingly, Cheryl had halted production, as we waited for the police to arrive. Feeling guilty for having disrupted the crime scene, I made sure no one else stepped out of the castle to further alter anything. Cheryl, Adam, and I mutually decided it would be best not to say anything to the others until the police had arrived and we knew the identity of the man at the bottom of the pool.

Cheryl assembled the cast and crew in the dining hall, giving out minimal information. Lunch had been provided for us, a similar semblance of the salad bar and sandwiches we'd had the evening before. I felt as if I was on pins and needles about the victim. Who was he? What had happened? Was his death connected to our being in the castle?

I made my way to Scott, quietly hoping I could get in a discreet word with him.

Jessica was chatting happily away with him. "It was a bottle of rum," she said, running her fingers through her impossibly long silky blond hair. "I found it next to the little ship . . . the little toy ship that sits in the hallway on that ancient telephone booth . . . It is a telephone booth, isn't it?"

Scott nodded. "Yup, like a little phone kiosk or something."

Jessica giggled and grabbed Scott's arm. "Exactly! That's exactly what it is. I guess they used to sit there—in the little kiosk—and turn the crank, wait for the operator, I think."

They were chatting so amicably it annoyed me. I stood next to Scott, hoping to get his attention.

Jessica smiled at me. "I don't know how the rum is supposed to help me solve the murder, though."

Anxiety flooded my chest. Now we had a real dead body on our hands, not a cold case. Had it been a murder? Was there someone around us capable of that?

I'd heard noises coming from behind the bushes. What exactly were they? Voices? An altercation? Just rustling in the wind?

When had it happened? I'd spoken with Becca and Dr. Arch last night in front of the pool. What time had that been?

I glanced at Dr. Arch as he served himself a sandwich. He seemed quite content, even smiling and flirting with Ashley, the paranormal docent. He piled food onto his plate. Certainly, if he had a guilty conscience, it wasn't stopping his appetite at all.

Scott turned to me and asked. "What'd you find, G?"

I wanted to tell them exactly what I'd found, but I stuttered instead.

Scott frowned as he looked at me, then said to Jessica, "Uh, will you excuse us a second?"

Her shoulders hunched up a bit as she realized something was up. "Is everything all right?" She blinked rapidly as she surmised that neither Scott nor I was going to answer her. "Oh, I see Ashley." She pointed across the room, where Ashley was perusing the buffet table next to Dr. Arch. "I think I'll put together a little sandwich for myself and join her."

Jessica crossed the room toward the buffet table and as soon as she was out of earshot, I leaned into Scott.

He put his hand on the small of my back and pressed me into him. "What it is, G? What's wrong?"

For a moment, I wanted nothing more than to relish the warmth of his hand and hope that things were getting better for us. I squeezed my eyes shut and buried my face into his neck, inhaling his unique scent of cedar mixed with leather. Before I could tell Scott about the body, the sharp blast of a police siren permeated the thin windows.

The black-and-white had arrived.

Scott's body jerked sharply as he turned to the windows. "What's going on?"

"I found a body," I said to him as I walked toward the window.

The rest of the cast and crew seemed oddly uninterested in the police vehicle outside. Except Bert, the psychic, who joined me at the window. Outside, as the officer exited his vehicle, a woman with gray curly hair set in a bouffant rushed toward him.

"Who's that?" I asked.

Scott shrugged. "I don't know."

Ashley wandered over to us. "That's Gertrude. She sits on the board of the historical society that's in charge of renovating the castle. What's she all in a panic about?"

Outside, Cheryl, Gertrude, and the officer were discussing something in a very animated way.

Scott leaned in close to me. "Why don't you go outside and see if you can help?" he asked.

Cheryl had asked the cameraman and me to wait inside, as she didn't want the rest of the cast and crew to be alarmed. But sooner or later, the officer would want to take our statements, and as it was, I was chomping at the bit to talk to him.

I nodded. "All right. I'll go check in with Cheryl." I turned to exit the room, but Bert caught my arm.

"Georgia! Wait. It's not good," he said.

An ominous feeling filled my belly. "What isn't?" I asked.

"My vision. The man—" he said.

"How do you know about the man?" I asked.

Bert shrugged. "I had a vision. He drowned."

"Drowned? Come on. The pool is empty. There was no way he was drowned. He fell, maybe. Hit his head on the bottom of the pool."

But that didn't seem right. There hadn't been the tell-tale sign of blood. If he'd been alive when he fell, he would have bled . . .

The psychic grabbed both of my wrists. "Georgia, I'm telling you. I see water."

"All right," I said, pulling my wrists away from him. "I'll let the police know."

How could Bert have known about the body?

Had he overheard me? Or had the cameraman said anything to him? I rushed outside, happy to have an excuse to approach the officer and insert myself into the investigation.

The wind buffeted my face as the woman, Gertrude, stalked off. She glared at me as she whizzed past me back into the castle. The officer in charge was middle-aged with dark hair and a bushy mustache. He had a small paunch and stood with his legs apart and his arms folded. He was listening to Cheryl do a song and dance. He didn't seem at all impressed.

"Excuse me," I said.

The officer turned toward me, raising a hand to block the sun from his eyes.

"This is Georgia Thornton. She's the one who found the man," Cheryl said by way of introduction.

The officer nodded at me. "Miss, will you please show me where the man is?"

"The pool is around back," Cheryl said.

"You don't need to see him again, if you find it upsetting," the officer said.

"I'm all right," I said. "I used to work for SFPD."

The officer frowned, as if trying to make a connection

between my previous experience on the police force and my presence here at the castle. He said nothing, though he followed Cheryl and me around the castle toward the back grounds where the pool was. As we walked, I studied the dirt path leading up to the pool. It didn't seem to have any unusual disturbances, just regular foot traffic, along with various paw prints, likely squirrels or other small critters. There were also deep grooves along the path that I couldn't identify.

When we reached the pool, the officer peered over the side. "Is that how you found him?" he asked.

"Huh, no," I confessed. "He was facedown. I flipped him over."

The officer chewed on the inside of his cheek, annoyed. "You're not supposed to touch him, you know."

"Yes, I know that," I said.

He scowled at me. "As former SFPD, you should know better."

I shrugged. "I didn't know if he needed medical attention."

"All right. Well, I'll need your prints to put on record," he said.

"My prints are already on record, but I'm happy to go down to the police station and give them to you again."

He made a note in his notebook and mumbled something under his breath. He looked at Cheryl. "What's that package in the corner of the pool? Any idea? It looks new."

Cheryl nodded. "Our tech put it there yesterday. It was something Georgia was supposed to find."

The officer looked from Cheryl to me. "All right. I'm going to want to talk to the person who put it there."

"Of course," Cheryl agreed.

"And I'll have to take it into evidence," he added.

"I understand," Cheryl said. She turned to me. "I'll have to arrange something else for you."

I shrugged. Not knowing what was in the original package, I couldn't be happy or sad if it was replaced with something else. "That's fine," I said to her, then turned to the officer. "I wanted to tell you something else. Something the psychic said."

The officer frowned. "The psychic?"

I shrugged and glanced at Cheryl. "Have you explained to him what we're doing here?"

"Yes," she said. "I told him we're doing a paranormal TV show, a reality show, trying to solve the murder of Jane Reiner. The cold case in the castle."

He nodded. "Yeah, I've heard all about it. It's quite the talk in town."

"Well," I continued, "the psychic has some strange reason to think that the man in the pool drowned."

The officer straightened, fixing his eyes on me. "What reason?"

"He had a vision," I confessed.

The officer snickered. "Oh, right. Yeah. I'll go ahead and make a note of that," he said sarcastically.

I looked at the man at the bottom of the pool. "Any guess as to what the cause of death was?"

The officer said, "I don't know. It looks like he fell,

probably hit his head on the bottom of the pool, or broke his neck, or something."

"Not much blood down there," I said.

"Trauma to the head doesn't always mean blood," he countered.

"I suppose you'll have the coroner or ME take a look," I said.

The officer grunted.

An ominous feeling surfaced in my gut. "You are going to investigate, right?" I asked.

He shrugged. "Well, it looks like an obvious accident."

I glanced at Cheryl for support. She scowled at me, trying to ward me off. "Well, at least an autopsy," I insisted. "You'll have them do an autopsy, correct?"

"I'm waiting for the medical examiner right now. The next of kin need to be notified, and we'll go from there." He glanced at Cheryl. "I'll need to cordon off this area."

A look of panic crossed Cheryl's face. "For how long?"

"We'll see," he answered. He looked around back at the castle. "I suppose I'll need a list of everyone who was here last night."

Cheryl said, "Consider it done."

The officer turned to me. "And I'd like to speak with the man you were with when you found the body."

"Adam Flynn, our senior cameraman," Cheryl said. "He's inside. I can get him."

From the officer's shoulder-holstered radio came a chirp. He nodded at Cheryl as he momentarily stepped away from us. The sound of gravel crunching under tires, the telltale sound of a car approaching, made the officer wind his way back to the front of the castle.

Cheryl took advantage of the distraction and pulled me aside. "What are you doing with all those questions, Georgia? We don't want them to investigate. They'll shut us down. Just let them call it an accident."

"But Cheryl," I said. "What are the chances of it being an accident? We're investigating a cold case and somebody dies on the premises. It's pretty darn suspicious if you ask me."

"Well, no one is asking you," Cheryl hissed.

She was right. No one was asking me, and it stung. I'd been ousted by the San Francisco Police Department—not that I'd ever been a homicide detective—and now I was being ousted here.

But still . . . there must be a connection between this case and the cold case. It seemed the timing was too coincidental. Could this man have known anything about Jane's murder?

Had he known her? What was his connection to the castle?

"Who is he?" I asked Cheryl. "Do we even know that?"

"A groundskeeper," she said.

"A groundskeeper of the castle?"

She nodded. "That's what Gertrude, the lady who runs the historical society, said. She was anxious because when she went to call on him this morning at his cottage, he wasn't there. Apparently they always have coffee together in the mornings. Anyway, when she took her tour of the castle while we were waiting on the police, she identified him."

The officer returned with the crime scene crew in tow. The team unfolded themselves around the pool, some screeching down the ladder. The officer took my name and information. "We'll be in touch," he said, as a dismissal.

I glanced at Cheryl.

She grabbed my arm and dragged me back into the castle. "Let's get back inside before they put a stop to our filming."

The rest of the cast was still inside the dining room. When Cheryl and I entered, Scott came to my side immediately and put an arm around me. Cheryl called Adam over and told him to speak with the officer outside. Then she clapped her hands together and got the attention of the cast and crew.

"Folks, there's been an unfortunate accident on the grounds," she said.

I grumbled and she shot me a look so fierce it could have frozen the depths of hell—reminding me why I'd nicknamed her the Wicked Witch of the West when I'd first met her. Scott's grip around my shoulders tightened and he whispered, "Just breathe."

Cheryl cleared her throat. "The groundskeeper to the castle has had an accident—"

The room filled with gasps and chatter: "Oh, dear." "Is he all right?" "Nothing serious, I hope!"

Bert, the psychic, flashed me a disbelieving look. "It was no accident," he said under his breath.

Dr. Arch asked, "Is there something I can do?"

"Or perhaps my services are necessary?" Father Gabriel asked.

Cheryl held up a hand. "No, no. There's nothing to be done at this point. Except stay out of the way. The police are on site—"

"Police?" Jessica asked. "Why are the police here?"

Cheryl pressed her lips together and managed to look contrite. "The poor man fell into the empty pool outside, I'm afraid. The police are here to take his body away and notify his family."

Jack, the ghost hunter, shuddered. "I knew there was way too much paranormal activity on my EMF this morning!"

Ashley, the paranormal docent, shrieked, "You're right! Those readings were off the charts!"

Martha, the historian, let out an anxious wail, while Father Gabriel steadied her.

"Now, now," Cheryl said. "I don't think there's anything paranormal about this. The man simply had an accident. It's unfortunate, yes, but I wouldn't say that any kind of supernatural activity caused it."

Irritation prickled my neck. There was no way that groundskeeper had fallen into the pool accidentally. He was a groundskeeper of the castle. How many times had he pruned those roses and walked around that pool? It didn't seem likely to me that his death was accidental.

Cheryl let out an uncharacteristic nervous giggle. "Well, anyway, if there was something peculiar about it, we'll know soon enough, there are cameras everywhere." She motioned around her and suddenly it seemed like the walls had eyes. There were small automatic lenses hidden throughout the panels.

Instinctively I watched the cast's reaction. Had anyone just discovered their crime had been captured on camera? Sadly, the cast seemed more horrified to discover that we were secretly being filmed than to learn about the groundskeeper's demise.

Cheryl gave us a few minutes to wrap up our lunch and then instructed us to get touch-ups on our hair and makeup before proceeding with the rest of the filming. She meant to capitalize on any news leaks about the groundskeeper, and if all went well, use it for ratings.

Suddenly the cast and crew seemed energized to get back to work, leaving me wondering about the future of humanity.

Kyle approached me. "Ladies, on the third floor," he said. "That's where you'll go to get your touch-up."

"Third floor?" I asked.

He nodded at me, then turned to Scott. "Men are on the first floor, as usual." He scurried away before we could ask more questions.

Scott wrapped his finger through mine. "Are you okay, G?"

I nodded, feeling grateful for his attention. "I'm okay, but my gut is screaming. Something is up and we have to watch our backs."

Scott squeezed my hand before releasing it. "Be careful then," he said. "I'll see you in a few minutes."

The room was beginning to clear out and we separated in the hallway as he hurried off to the men's makeup area.

I made my way up the rickety steps to the third floor, suddenly feeling desperately alone.

The castle seemed colder than usual, and I tried not to let it get to me. The fact that no one wanted to investigate the poor groundskeeper's death was bothering me.

Instead, we were focusing on a cold case, but I knew everyone was more motivated by ratings than justice.

As I made my way up the staircase past the second floor, the steps became uneven. There were large gaping holes in the wood and I had to grip the banister and hoist myself up several steps at a time in order to get to the third floor.

When I arrived, I realized the floor was deserted.

Where was everyone?

How was I supposed to get my hair and makeup done if no one was up here?

"Hello?" I called out.

No answer.

I walked down the corridor. The floor was rotted, creaking and groaning as I put my weight on it. The walls were full of water stains, and the passageway reeked of mold. It was eerily quiet and creepy at the same time. Then, I heard urgent whispers, two voices, but I couldn't make out who they were or what they were saying.

What's going on?

I rapidly made my way toward the noise. It sounded like men's voices, but that was wrong. The men were downstairs. This was supposed to be ladies only. I hurried toward the voices, coming from behind a closed door.

I gripped the knob and pushed open the door. There was a loud splintering and shattering sound, then the floor gave away. My body jolted furiously, and I unwillingly yielded to the sickening sensation of falling, like poor Alice through the looking glass.

Seven

....

My life flashed before my eyes as the shocking sensation of falling through the air ricocheted through my body. I screamed and flailed for something to stop my fall. Then a scorching pain seared through my leg as rotten wood stabbed and ripped at my thigh.

I roared in pain as I dangled in midair, my leg painfully pinched between two boards. Father Gabriel and Dr. Arch rushed out of the room at the end of the hallway.

"Georgia! Georgia! Hang on!" Dr. Arch yelled, as he ran toward me.

Both men grabbed ahold of my arms and hoisted me upward.

The wood tore deeper into my flesh and I yelped, "My leg!"

Dr. Arch gingerly pulled the wood back and freed me.

They yanked me back onto the third floor. The house seemed to shudder as I rolled onto the rotted floor, and then another loud rumbling resounded.

"It's going to give way!" Father Gabriel yelled.

They quickly dragged me forward, toward the staircase. Then a thunderous crashing burst forth as if the entire third floor was about to collapse around us. I scrambled to my feet, a hot stabbing pain shooting through my thigh as we raced toward the stairwell. We tussled headlong down the steps to the second floor just as what remained of the hallway on the third floor gave way onto the second floor.

We stood in shock, huddled together in the stairwell, our arms covering each other as best we could. When the wood planks seemed to stop raining on us, Father Gabriel said, "Good Lord. Georgia, are you all right?"

I felt lightheaded and dizzy, but before I could answer, one of the crew members rushed up the stairs. "What's going on? What happened?"

He was followed closely by Scott, who shouted. "Georgia! Georgia!" He reached out for me and grabbed my wrist.

I collapsed into his arms, the burning in my leg making me feel nauseous.

"Let's get off the staircase," Dr. Arch said.

Scott took in our damaged surroundings. "Holy smokes. You all could have been killed."

We descended the stairs toward the lobby, where Cheryl stood with her arms folded across her chest and an angry scowl on her face.

I left a trail of blood in my wake. We must have looked a fright because Cheryl didn't scold us; she only snapped her fingers at one of the show runners, a girl with dyed purple hair and multiple piercings in her nose.

"Get Jose!" Cheryl said, pointing at my leg. "Georgia needs attention."

The girl with the purple hair raced off.

The pain in my thigh sizzled and I searched for a place to rest. Scott's grip around my waist tightened as he sensed my discomfort and I clutched at him.

"Do I need to call 911?" Cheryl asked, with an expression on her face that seemed like she was in more pain than I was.

"I can take a look," Dr. Arch said. "Let's go over to the living room area and see if you can lie down a minute."

Scott frowned. "I thought you were a forensic archaeologist."

Dr. Arch smiled. "I only play one on TV. I'm a podiatrist."

I would have laughed, but the pain in my thigh was beginning to overwhelm me and my knees buckled.

Scott caught me, and between him and Dr. Arch, they helped me out of the room.

Down the hall, the girl with the purple hair retuned with Jose in tow. He wore torn blue jeans and a white T-shirt. He had a tattoo of a snake that ran the length of his arm and hand. He gripped a red first aid box in his hand, but the effect of the tattoo looked as if the snake held the box in its teeth.

"First aid?" Jose asked, looking at my leg.

Dr. Arch nodded. "Let's get her recumbent and take a look."

Scott set up a sleeping bag for me, while Jose pulled out a pair of scissors from the first aid box. As Jose cut away my jeans, Dr. Arch sanitized his hands.

My leg throbbed and I closed my eyes to distract myself from the never-ending stream of blood that pooled around my leg.

Cheryl stood over me, her hands on her hips. "Georgia, what were you doing up there? I thought everyone knew that the third floor was off limits!"

"Kyle sent me up there," I moaned. "He said hair and makeup had been relocated . . ."

Cheryl reddened and looked around the room. "Where is Kyle? He knows better. Nobody should've sent you upstairs."

Dr. Arch tsked as he looked at my leg. "It's deep. We're going to have to do stitches."

My heart thumped through my chest.

Stitches?

Jose agreed, then said, "Georgia, we have to clean the wound. It's going to sting."

Scott squeezed my hand. "Don't you have any pain relief in there?"

"Give her something local," Cheryl said. "I don't want her all dopey, then I'd have to give up the whole day of filming."

"Some heart you have," Scott scoffed.

Cheryl blew him off. "She's tough."

"I can do a local," Jose said as he prepared a syringe.

Cheryl tapped her foot. "I guess we can film some confessionals in the meantime. So we don't burn too much of our schedule."

Scott's face turned red. "You'll excuse us if we're more concerned about Georgia bleeding all over the place instead of your bloody schedule."

Cheryl pursed her lips and said nothing.

Jose pinched a bit of my leg and gave me the shot. "How did this happen?" he asked.

"The wood flooring upstairs is so deteriorated that I literally stepped right through the floor," I said, through gritted teeth.

Jose gave a shudder. "This place is giving me the creeps. I'm glad the crew doesn't have to sleep here." He suddenly looked at Cheryl, fear in his eyes, as if he realized he shouldn't have mentioned a vulnerability in front of her.

Cheryl, for her part, snickered, then waved a hand around, indicating to Jose and Dr. Arch that she thought they were taking too long.

Jose tested the local anesthesia by pinching at my leg. "Do you feel anything?"

"Not really," I admitted. He poured some disinfectant on my open wound and I yelped. "I felt that."

Jose grimaced. "Sorry."

I took a deep breath and decided to focus on something else. "If the third floor was off limits, what were Dr. Arch and Father Gabriel doing up there?" I asked.

Dr. Arch frowned. "We weren't on the third floor. We only came up when we heard you screaming." He turned to Jose. "Can you take her blood pressure, please? If she's stable, I'll do the stitches now."

Jose took hold of my left arm and wrapped the blood pressure cuff around it.

"You and Father Gabriel were on the third floor," I insisted. "I heard you both arguing."

Scott shook his head. "No, G. The men were sent over into the west wing for hair and makeup, not the third floor."

"Blood pressure is stable," Jose said.

"Can you feel this?" Dr. Arch asked.

He was pressing my leg with something but I couldn't tell what. I tried to prop myself up to take a look, but with Jose holding one arm and Scott the other, it seemed impossible.

"Not really," I said. "But I hope it won't hurt like the disinfectant."

Dr. Arch nodded. "You feel something? Pressure?"

"Yes," I said.

"Not hot or cold?" he asked.

"No."

"All right," he said. "Just relax a moment."

I closed my eyes and tried not to think about my leg. Something was curious about the whole situation. Why had Kyle sent me up there? Had he intended for me to get injured or worse? We'd always had our little catty differences. But certainly Kyle wouldn't try to kill me, would he?

And what had Dr. Arch and Father Gabriel been doing up there? More important—why deny they'd been there?

"You're lying. I know you're up to something," I whispered.

Dr. Arch said, "Hold tight, Georgia. I'm almost done now."

Jose let out a whistle. "Doc, you're good. Those look great."

Scott patted my arm. "You okay?"

I sighed. "I'm okay."

I was more bothered about Dr. Arch lying than about the cut on my leg. I'd had plenty of scrapes and bruises in my life.

Suddenly, the woman from the historical society, Gertrude, rushed into the room. She had an angry expression on her face and Cheryl raced over to intercept her. They had a heated exchange, the woman's curly bouffant bouncing as she spoke in rapid-fire words with Cheryl.

Then the woman dismissed Cheryl and rushed over to me. "What were you doing on the third floor? That's off limits. We're going to have a masquerade fundraising ball after the show is over, and we can't have the place destroyed," she yelled at me. "The board won't have it. As soon as I tell them that you've ruined the castle, they're going to vote the show off the premises," she screamed.

Cheryl held up her hand. "Now, now, Gertrude, let's not get carried away. The show can repair the damages on the third floor."

"It's absolutely impossible," the woman screamed.

"You can't get enough equipment to go up there. You can't even find anybody to do the work up there. We've been trying to renovate the castle forever. I told you those floors were unsafe."

"I understand," Cheryl said. "There was a mix-up. One of our makeup crew." She looked around the room for Kyle. "Where is he?" She turned to one of the sound engineers, who seemed like he was deliberately trying to keep out of her way. "What are you doing standing around, Murphy? Go get Kyle right now. Tell him I need to see him." The sound engineer careened out of the room, not wanting to fan Cheryl's anger any further.

"I'm going to call an emergency board meeting," Gertrude said. "I hope you're satisfied. You came here under certain conditions, and you haven't upheld your end of the bargain." She jutted out a finger at Cheryl. "I want you, and your crew, and your cast out of here in the morning."

Cheryl made a face. "Now, now. I'm sure we can straighten this out. It's all a big misunderstanding," she said. She attempted to put a conciliatory arm out toward Gertrude, but the woman only stepped back, her face red and angry.

"Morning time. In fact, I shouldn't even give you until morning. You should pack your things up right now," she said. "After all, what happened with poor Walter, it's . . ." The woman's hand fluttered to her collarbone, and she plucked the gold necklace she wore. "I knew this was bad luck having you here. First the birds, and then Walter. Now the third floor? Don't you see what's happening?" she asked.

Good Lord. Was the woman about to tell us that we were cursed?

"They're all unrelated incidences," Scott said, standing up and squaring his shoulders to her. "The black birds were just migrating, and what happened to the poor groundskeeper has nothing to do with the third floor. Georgia was misinformed. She went up there thinking . . ."

Gertrude put him off. "I don't need to hear from you, young man," she said, snarling.

I made an attempt to prop myself up, but pain shot through my leg. I yelped and Jose put a restraining hand back on my shoulder. "You need to rest," he said. "Don't move."

I groaned, settling my head down on the sleeping bag.

Gertrude and Cheryl continued to argue, as Cheryl skillfully ushered her out of the room.

"I want you out of here," Gertrude repeated. "All of you, out, out, out!"

Cheryl whispered something I couldn't hear in a hushed urgent tone. I wanted to be part of it. I wanted to know what was going on.

Could it be true that our show would be cleared out of the castle?

Next, Kyle floated into the room. He rushed over to me, screaming, "Georgia! I just heard! I'm so sorry!" Then spotted the blood that stained the sleeping bag under my leg and turned away repulsed. "Ah! Blood!"

Dr. Arch chuckled and left the room.

Kyle made a big show of covering his eyes. "Georgia. I didn't mean to cause you any trouble. I swear!" he said.

"Why did you tell me to go to the third floor?" I asked.

He looked sheepish. "I got a text. Somebody said they were moving the women up to the third floor because they wanted the north wing for the shoot, and I was to tell you to go up there."

"Well, what about the other women?" I asked. "Did you tell them?"

He shrugged. "No. I'm only assigned to you. Clarissa has the others. Anyway, I was running late. I had to rush out to pack up my makeup bag. I thought Clarissa would notify everyone else. Where is she, by the way? I swear that woman is always on a perpetual coffee break!"

"Can I see your phone?" I asked.

He handed me his phone. "Yeah, have a look, but it's gone."

"Gone?" I said. We scrolled through his text log.

"I don't know what happened to it. It was right there, but I can't remember the number. I think it was a local area code," he said.

"Well, who has your number?" I asked.

He shrugged. "Everyone. It's posted on the front board."

I got the sickening feeling I'd just been set up, but by whom?

More important, why?

Eight

·················

As the burning in my leg went from a roar to a dull ache, the fatigue seemed to weigh heavily on my eyelids. I felt myself drifting off, when suddenly a young woman I hadn't seen before floated into the room. She didn't have any piercings or tattoos, which made it unlikely that she was part of the crew.

And yet . . . something about her was so familiar.

There was a kindness to her and she seemed to radiate a white light. She came closer to me, concern in her face.

Was she a nurse?

"Will you help me, Georgia?" she asked.

I struggled to sit up. "Help you? Help you how? Who are you?"

The young woman smiled. "I'm Jane. I need justice. I want you to help me get justice."

I searched around the room for the cameras. Was this a setup? Where was Cheryl? Were they filming this with some small camera concealed in the woman's clothing?

"Sure," I said cautiously. "I can help you. Why don't you tell me what happened? Who killed you?"

A sad and forlorn expression crossed Jane's face. "I wish I knew!" she said. "It happened so fast. I heard voices, and then an awful fear overtook me. As if my body knew what was about to happen before my mind did. That moment . . . when your heart races and you know . . . I was turning around. It couldn't have taken that long for me to turn around . . . and yet I never did get to see who it was. That moment, though, it's suspended. It's suspended into all eternity."

Her voice warbled and she seemed to fade a bit, like someone turning down a light.

What kind of illusion is this?

I looked around the room again. Was she an image? A projection of sorts?

"The hit was so hard," Jane said, rubbing at the back of her head. "I blacked out and that's all I remember."

"Where were you when they killed you?" I asked.

"My room. On the third floor. I'd just finished writing a letter to mother. I so wanted to go home. I knew something awful would happen. The boys here at the home were so terrible. I knew it was a matter of time. And then after I saw . . . well, I wasn't supposed to see it . . ."

"Saw what? What did you see?" I asked.

A voice came into the room from down the hall. Jane seemed to flicker.

"Wait! Wait! What did you see?" I struggled to grab ahold of her, but my hand went through the air.

She was gone.

Someone was shaking my shoulder. My eyes fluttered and I was surprised to look up into Scott's face.

"Georgia! Are you okay?" he asked. "It seemed like you were having a bad dream." His brow furrowed and a look of concern crossed his face. He leaned into me, his face close to mine. "You're trembling. Does your leg hurt? Do you need me to ask for some painkillers for you?"

I rubbed at my eyes. It had been a dream. Just a dream. *It didn't mean a thing.*

INT. LIBRARY DAY

Martha and Father Gabriel are seated in matching high-back chairs. They are looking into the camera. Martha's chestnut-colored hair has been styled so that it's pulled back away from her face, clearly emphasizing the look of concern she is wearing. Her legs are crossed. She jiggles her foot nervously as she speaks, her black-and-white polka-dotted skirt fluttering around her ankles. Father Gabriel, in contrast, looks relaxed and confident. He is dressed in a traditional black cassock; around his neck is a wooden cross dangling on a rough rope as worn by priests in his order.

MARTHA
(*smiles*) Hello, my name is Martha. I decided to come on *Cold Case in the Castle* because I thought my vast background as a historian would aid in solving the murder of Jane Reiner. You see, Jane was murdered in 1968. That was a turbulent time in the United States. (*She glances at Father Gabriel.*) And having lived through that time, I think you and I understand it better than the other contestants.

FATHER GABRIEL
(*laughing*) Now, dear, didn't we say we wouldn't use their youth and inexperience against them?

MARTHA
Right. You're right, Gabriel. Everyone has to start somewhere. I suppose what I meant to say is that for a woman Jane's age, attempting to make a new life for herself as a librarian, here in this castle . . . well, the challenges were very steep indeed. And while it was unusual for a young woman to

be employed in the state reform jurisdiction, Jane was. She must have been very brave indeed.

FATHER GABRIEL
(*clearing his throat*) In fact, .in 1968 there were only a handful of women in the castle at all.

MARTHA
That's right. There was the cook and only two teachers.

FATHER GABRIEL
That's not to say, no women visiting the castle. Plenty of women came on visiting day. Mothers, sisters, even girlfriends. But no other young women lived here.

MARTHA
(*nodding enthusiastically*) Exactly! You understand my point. Between the two of us, we are uniquely positioned to solve this murder.

FATHER GABRIEL
(*turning to the camera*) But you must vote for us, dear viewer!

MARTHA
(frowns suddenly) What number do we tell
them to call?

CAMERAMAN (O.S.)
We'll scroll a number at the bottom of the
screen.

MARTHA AND FATHER GABRIEL
(smiling widely) Just call the number at the
bottom of the screen!

Cheryl flew into the room. "Georgia! How's the leg? Can you walk? I've stalled as much as I can, but with the audience live voting I can only delay so long."

Scott helped me to my feet and I tested some weight on my leg by gently bouncing up and down on it. "Uh . . . I think I'm okay."

The truth was my leg still hurt something awful, but I was antsy to get going as well. I certainly didn't want to stay put and risk another screwy nightmare.

Cheryl nodded and patted my arm. "Atta girl. I must say our hidden cameras caught it all. We have an amazing shot of you dangling between floors. It looks downright spooky. It'll play great on the promos. Should yield us some great dividends!"

"You know what would yield some great dividends, at

least in terms of goodwill, is if you pretended you cared about Georgia for just a minute," Scott fumed.

Cheryl scoffed. "Don't be so melodramatic. I care about her." She pinched my arm, getting me to yelp in agreement.

But my mind was elsewhere. "Hidden cameras?" I asked.

Cheryl frowned. "Don't worry about them. It's best when you all don't act silly and preen around."

"I'm not going to preen around," I said, trying not to be offended. "I mean to ask, what else did the cameras show? Were you able to get Dr. Arch and Father Gabriel on film on the third floor?"

Cheryl shook her head. "No. We don't have any film of anyone on the third floor except for you."

How could that be?

"What about at the pool? Did the cameras catch anything on the groundskeeper—"

Cheryl waved an impatient hand around. "Okay, if you're well enough to poke your nose into that investigation, you're well enough to get on with filming." She stalked off without answering my question to corral the cast and crew.

Soon it was showtime again. We'd been assembled in the library. Kyle rushed over to me and primped my hair.

"Girl!" Kyle said. "You really need a full do-over. I don't know what Cheryl thinks I can do in ten minutes, but you are a mess."

"Thanks," I muttered.

He put an end to my protests by applying lip lacquer—and as every woman knows it's impossible to talk while someone is telling you to stretch your lips.

"This color brightens you up. You're so pale right now you look like you saw a ghost."

The image of Jane in my dream came to mind, but before I could reply Scott said, "Maybe she's lost too much blood?"

Dr. Arch glanced over. "No, no. She only needed a few stitches. She's fine. Right, Georgia?"

"Still, she should probably eat or something, right?" Scott asked, his brow furrowing as he evaluated me.

One of the crew members blew into the room and thrust a package into my hand. "This is what you were supposed to find at the bottom of the pool," he said.

I took the package from him and looked inside. "What is it?" I asked.

Scott peeked over my shoulder. "Hopefully a couple of PowerBars."

I wrinkled my nose. "I'm not that hungry."

He wrinkled his nose back at me, then leaned forward so his forehead pressed against mine. "You really don't know what's good for you, do you?"

I smiled, seizing the moment to look into his dark eyes and relish his closeness.

"With any luck they gave you a laptop," he said, pointing at the package. "I found a network card."

Kyle pushed Scott aside. "Excuse *moi*, I wasn't finished

here!" He spritzed something cold on my face and mumbled to himself.

Then Harris entered the room and made a big show of taking center stage. Kyle abandoned me and flocked over to him. He waved a stiff clothes brush over Harris's shoulder, flicking away imaginary debris. Harris came to life under the attention.

The rest of the cast streamed into the room, flashing me looks of concern and murmuring good wishes. I noted that most everyone held a black leather sack, much like what I held. I realized that I'd been so concerned with finding the groundskeeper and then my subsequent accident that I hadn't really bothered to figure out what everyone had found on the treasure hunt.

Jack and Bert inched closer to me.

"Are you all right?" Bert asked. "I had a terrible headache earlier and feared you might be in danger."

I sighed. "What good is being psychic if you only get the warning after the fact," I fired at him.

He looked hurt. "I'm sorry," he said. "Sometimes I wonder the same thing myself."

Jack dismissed the admonition and asked, "What did you find?"

I pulled out a device from the sack. It was black with a red dial and something resembling a prong hanging from it. Definitely not a laptop. "I have no idea."

Jack's eyes widened. "Oh, good! A voltmeter! We need one of those."

I wondered who exactly was the "we" he was referring

to when Cheryl called out, "Places everyone." She put on a headset and scrambled to the back of the room saying, "Ready in five, four, three, two, one."

Harris stood in front of us, his arms held in a dramatic pose. "Well, ladies and gentlemen, you've all completed your first successful treasure hunt. It's unclear whether the item you have retrieved will be useful in solving the mystery or not, but one thing is clear: Each item can only go so far. Some of you were lucky enough to find a laptop." With that, he glanced at the FBI profiler, Karen Kenley, and smiled. "However, a laptop is no good without a battery." He quirked an eyebrow in Father Gabriel's direction. "You all will find that the key to solving this mystery will be to work together."

I looked over at Scott. He had a network card. It was clear that if we could work our way into Karen's graces, we might get a laptop or a battery from Father Gabriel.

Harris proceeded with his monologue, and I poked at Scott. "Who has what? Do you know?"

He shook his head back and forth. "I only know that Jessica got a bottle of rum, and now what Harris just revealed."

An unnerving feeling zipped through my stomach when he mentioned Jessica. He seemed to be spending a lot of time with her, or was that just my overactive imagination? I searched his eyes for anything that might reveal an attraction to her, but he only flashed me a goofy grin and then motioned over to Bert.

Bert pulled out a box of chocolates from his leather pouch and wiggled them at me suggestively.

I shook my head. "So what?" I asked.

"He probably wants the voltmeter you found," Scott whispered.

"And what, I get chocolates in exchange?"

He shrugged. "Well, what about Jack? He's got the DNA kit, I think."

There was probably only one person who could make use of a DNA kit, and that would be Karen. If I could get the DNA kit from Jack, then perhaps I could convince Karen to swap the laptop with me. We already knew Scott had the network card, so together, at least we might be able to get some information online.

Scott nodded. "It's a good plan."

As soon as Harris dismissed us, I approached Jack. Out of the corner of my eye, I saw Scott approach Jessica, and I fought the urge to follow him and eavesdrop on their conversation.

"Jack, you have a DNA kit?" I asked hopefully.

He nodded. "I don't know what I'm supposed to do with this."

"Are you interested in a trade?" I asked.

He looked at me. "What have you got?"

I showed him the voltmeter.

"Very interesting," he said. "Yes, I'd be interested. Do you know how to work this thing?" He glanced down at the DNA kit.

"I think I might know somebody who does," I said. We made a fair trade and shook on it.

Bert asked me, "Would you like a piece of chocolate?"

I laughed. "No, thank you."

He said, "I wouldn't mind giving these to your friend. Is she around?"

"Becca?" I asked him.

"Yes," he answered.

"She's not here. She's gone to help my dad with the almond harvest," I said.

"Oh." He made a face as if he was trying to mask his disappointment.

Around us, people were wheeling and dealing for different items. "Somebody else might be interested in the chocolate," I said.

Bert shrugged. "Well, I don't know what I would do with a laptop or even a battery. I might as well just hold on to the chocolates and just not distract myself. Maybe I can find a quiet corner to camp out in and meditate."

I shrugged. It's not as if I believed he was really psychic, but if he was, then certainly he was in no need of a laptop or a network card. People began to leave the room. Alliances were being formed. I saw Father Gabriel talk with Dr. Arch and exchange two items. My uneasiness grew. I needed to get on with things.

"I'm sorry, Bert. I need to go. Thank you, Jack, for the trade." Jack wiggled his eyebrows at me and gave me a little mock salute.

I headed off, determined to intercept Karen before she

left the room. "Karen," I said, "I have a DNA kit I thought you might be interested in."

She scowled at me. "Well, sure, if you're giving it away."

"Giving it away?" I said, "No, no. I was hoping you'd be interested in trading the laptop."

She laughed. "No way would I trade the laptop."

"Well, it's probably no good to you without a network card or a battery."

She gave me a smug smile. "I have both."

I tried to hide my surprise. There was no way she had the network card. I knew Scott had it, but I asked anyway, "You do?"

"Sure. Dr. Arch just traded a flashlight for a battery from the good father, and Jessica has agreed to loan me her network card."

"Jessica has a network card?" I asked.

But it couldn't be—hadn't Scott told me she won a bottle of rum, and I knew Scott had the network card. Had the cast been supplied with two cards? What was going on?

Karen brushed past me. "If you'll excuse me, we have a little research to do." She walked quickly out of the room, leaving me with my jaw agape.

A pit formed in my stomach. Could Scott have traded the network card for a bottle of rum?

I followed Karen out, searching for Scott. I found him sitting in the library perusing some of the books. "Hey, what's up?" I asked.

He smiled at me. "Nothing, just checking out a few books, see if I can figure anything out."

"Do you still have the network card?" I asked.

"No," he said. "I traded for a bottle of rum."

"What? I thought we agreed—"

He held up a hand, looking a bit sad. "Well, Karen wasn't going to give up the laptop, so I figured it was kind of pointless. This way, at least we can get drunk."

"Scott, I traded the voltmeter for the DNA kit. I was going to try to work Karen for the laptop. It was useless to her without the network card."

Scott blinked at me. "I'm sorry, Georgia. I didn't think. I figured your leg was probably hurting and this"— he waved the bottle at me—"might take the edge off."

I wanted to be angry. In fact, I was angry, but I didn't want to show it. I knew Scott was trying his hardest. Wasn't he?

Or was he really just trying to get off the show?

A wave of sadness overwhelmed me, and I felt lost at the same time. I picked at some peeling paint on the wall. "Do you want to go? Is that it?" I asked him.

"What do you mean?"

"Be voted off the show. Tonight's the first elimination."

He shrugged. "No, nothing like that. I think we have a good chance of winning. You do, anyway."

"Not without any tools," I said.

"You have tools. You've got a DNA kit."

I shrugged. "I don't think it's worth anything to me. I

would have rather had the laptop and the network card, but now we've got a bottle of rum."

Jack and Bert entered the library holding on to the chocolates and the voltmeter. They were followed closely by a cameraman. Jack's voltmeter was lighting up. "Hey gang. We followed the current over here. Lot of electricity sparking in this room," Jack said.

Maybe my temper was lighting up the voltmeter.

Jack went over to the window and the voltmeter started to spike. "Lots of activity indeed," he said. He scanned the walls. Bert took a seat next to Scott and held out the box of chocolates to him. Together, they perused for the best ones.

"I like the soft centers," Jack said.

Scott smirked. "That works out well. I like the nut and chews myself." He popped open the rum.

Despair swarmed me. I no longer knew in which direction to turn. Scott didn't really seem interested in figuring out the case, and Bert and Jack were off on a paranormal deep end. I knew I didn't trust Dr. Arch, nor did I trust Father Gabriel, and yet they were likely teamed up in another part of the castle colluding against Scott and me.

An idea struck. I needed to make an alliance with them!

Nine

....

slunk down the hallway—only with my bad leg, my slinking probably looked more menacing than graceful. Still, I was as quiet as I could be, hoping to eavesdrop on Karen and Dr. Arch. After a moment, Scott joined me in the hallway.

So much for discretion.

Together we made our way down a long corridor. There were several large photographs on the wall. One of a crew of about fifty boys ranging from age eight to eighteen, all in uniform, all with sour expressions on their faces. Another photograph was of a gentleman in late middle age with a large handlebar mustache and donning a hat complete with a white plume on it.

Both photos gave me the heebie-jeebies, as if the people

in them were watching Scott and me creep down the corridor.

We passed the small phone kiosk with the toy ship on it where Jessica had found the rum, and I involuntarily grunted.

Scott touched my arm. "I'm sorry. Please don't be mad at me."

I shrugged, halfheartedly. "I'm not mad at you."

He said, "I felt so bad. Jessica started to cry, and I didn't know what to do. She was so upset and she thought having the network card would help."

I glared at him. "I thought having the network card would help also."

"I know. I'm sorry," he said.

"If I had balled my eyes out, would you have given it to me?" I asked sarcastically. I regretted my tone as soon as the words were out of my mouth.

Why did I have to be so mean?

Certainly that wasn't a promising strategy for winning back his heart.

But instead of being upset, Scott gave me a lopsided smile. "You don't cry about much, do you, Georgia?"

Was that a good thing?

We came upon a drawing room with a large brick fireplace that was the focal point of the room. There were several round tables scattered through the room. Settled at one were Dr. Arch, Jessica, Ashley, and Karen, all heads down leaning over a laptop.

Scott gave me a nod, and led the way into the room.

As soon as we walked in, the cameraman panned toward us, then Dr. Arch covered the screen. "What are you doing in here?" Dr. Arch demanded.

Scott held up the bottle of rum and give it a little jiggle. "Wondering if you wanted a drink."

The doctor laughed. "If it was good Scotch, I might be tempted."

Karen flicked her black hair, securing it over her left ear, away from her face. "Ah, you want a peek at the screen, don't you?"

Scott shrugged. "Well, if we can all work together, we might be able to figure something out."

"We haven't really found anything," Karen said. "Not anything past what we already know, anyway. Jane Reiner was a librarian in training here at the school in 1968, wherein she was murdered and the case has never been resolved."

"Who were the prime suspects?" I asked.

Karen blinked at me.

"That's just it," Jessica said. "There weren't really any suspects. They figured it was somebody at the school but we don't know for sure. We don't have access to the police reports."

I had access to old police reports, didn't I? I could call in a favor with some of my old colleagues over at the San Francisco Police Department, but I no longer had a phone. "Can I send an email?" I asked them.

Dr. Arch shrugged, "Sure, why not? Three minutes because we've got low battery."

"Who's got the power cord?" I asked.

"No one. They didn't provide us with a power cord and the network card has limited time on it, too," Jessica whined. She eyed the bottle of rum longingly as if she realized she had made a bad trade.

Scott laughed and took a swig of rum complete with a pirate-style "Argh."

They pushed the laptop toward me and I quickly fired off an email to some old friends asking them for the details of the case if they could come up with them. As soon as I hit send, the email server pinged and an unde-liverable message appeared on the screen.

Frustrated, I let my mind wander, hoping for an epiph-any. My thoughts drifted back to the groundskeeper, Walter, I'd found in the pool last night. What connection had he had to the first murder, if any? How long had he been groundskeeper? Would the officer who arrived to take the information be willing to share any files with me?

I itched to try to search the Internet for information, but I didn't even know the groundskeeper's last name. Instead, I Googled the historical society for the castle. A biography of Gertrude Silverman came up. I scanned the website for staff photos, to see if I could find Walter's last name.

I was distinctly aware of the cameraman moving behind me to capture my search. He was sure to record everything, especially the negotiations with Karen and Dr. Arch. A moment later, Father Gabriel and Martha, the historian, found us in the drawing room.

"Any information?" Father Gabriel asked.

"Not much," Dr. Arch confessed. "It seems that we're going around in circles."   .

The priest paced the room. "I must say I find this place concerning. Disturbingly so. It feels as if there's so many spirits about, lost souls." He looked saddened. "If only the producers would let me free these lost souls."

"How would you do that?" Scott asked, handing him the bottle of rum.

"It's rather involved," Father Gabriel said. Then he surprised me by actually taking a hearty swig. He made a face after swallowing the rum. "Uck. I prefer wine," he said, wiping his mouth with the back of his hand.

We all laughed.

From down the hall came a loud clattering and a ghostly scream. The hair on the back of my neck stood on end as we all scrambled toward the noise. Father Gabriel sprang to attention and began to chant something to Saint Michael or Saint George. I couldn't keep up with him. I was the last one out of the room. Even hobbling, the pain in my leg was debilitating. In the hallway, we ran into Jack and Bert. Bert looked pale and Jack was flushed red.

"What's going on?" Scott demanded.

"We found something in the library," Bert said.

Ashley, the paranormal docent, raced ahead of us. "Quick, who has the voltmeter?"

"I do," Jack said. Together they tore off toward the library.

"I need my scented oils!" Father Gabriel said. He pulled a rosary out of his pocket. "Some holy water, and salt. We need to clean the doorways!" he yelled, racing after Bert and Jack.

Next to me, Scott chortled.

"It's not funny," I said. "They believe."

"I know they do," he answered. He passed me the rum. "You need to relax."

"I can't relax," I said. "I'm sure the groundskeeper's death is connected."

"How so?" he asked.

"I don't know, a feeling. Maybe I'm psychic, too."

Scott wrapped his arms around me. "I hope you're not still mad at me."

I buried my face into his chest and inhaled his scent. "I told you. I'm not mad at you," I said.

"Are you sad?" he asked, pausing. I felt myself stiffen in his arms and he must have felt it, too, because he asked, "About us, I mean?"

"Yes," I agreed. "Kind of sad. I wish things could go back to the way they were."

He sighed. "Me, too." After a moment, he said, "I'm trying to get better. Georgia, you have to believe me."

"I do," I said, putting my hand on the base of his neck and pulling his face toward mine.

From behind, two of the crew practically trampled over us trying to get down the hallway. When one cameraman

stopped and filmed Scott's and my embrace, we disen-
tangled from each other and followed the commotion over
to the library. As soon as I walked in, the first thing to hit
me was the wonderful smell of musty books. It took all
my willpower not to wander over to the shelf and start
examining titles, but at one of the tables in the center of
the room, there was a Ouija board, and seated in front of
it was Ashley, the paranormal docent. Around her Jack
and Bert crowded in. It seemed like the thing to do, so
Scott and I leaned in as well.

The overhead lights flickered, and suddenly what little
power we had in the room went out.

Ashley screamed. "Oh, no! Here we go! I told you the
spirits are angry with us! Look what happened to
Georgia!"

The only light left in the room came from the windows, but a summer storm was brewing and dark clouds
rumbled in, leaving us in relative darkness.

The historian, Martha, let out a little yelp. "This can't
be real!"

"Who's got the flashlight?" I asked.

"I think Father Gabriel has it," Scott said.

Father Gabriel fumbled for the light and shone it at the
Ouija board. Ashley had both hands on the dial and her
wrists were flung around in all directions as she followed
whatever moved her, be it a spirit or her own mind.

"It's in the letters?" Jack asked. "What letters?"

"Must be these letters," Jessica said. "The letters of
the Ouija board."

"May the spirit of the archangel Michael guide any souls lingering in this realm over to where they belong," Father Gabriel prayed.

"Father! Don't!" Ashley pleaded. "You can't dismiss these spirits until they tell us what they need to say."

"It won't work anyway," Jack said. "The moon is waxing. The spirits won't be cleared during that phase. We need a waning moon."

"It's in the letters? Huh?" Scott asked. "What if it means something besides the letters of the Ouija board?"

"Like what?" Jack asked. "Like the writing's on the wall?"

An awful shock jolted through my body as I remembered my dream. In the dream, Jane had talked about her mother. About something she'd seen. "Could it be letters Jane wrote home?" I asked.

Suddenly a wind howled through the room as if a window had been opened. Several books tumbled to the floor in a loud crash.

Next to me, Martha screamed and reached out to grab ahold of Scott.

"It's okay," he soothed.

One book flew open, the pages fluttering.

"It's a sign!" Ashley said. "She's trying to tell us something!"

"Maybe it's just a draft," I said. "The castle is full of drafts." Although mostly I suspected the Ouija board and flying book were part of a dramatic setup, courtesy of Cheryl.

The cast crowded around the books. The only ones who didn't were Scott, Martha, and me. Martha clung to Scott like he was her newfound best friend. He gave her a reassuring pat on the shoulder. "It's okay. Keep breathing." To me, he winked and said, "We always have the rum to fall back on."

A flash of lightning illuminated the room, then the ominous sound of thunder claps. A cloud broke apart and rain began pounding on the window. Martha squeaked and grabbed Scott tighter.

"Why is it flipping from page seventeen back to page ninety-seven?" Jessica asked. "Does it mean something?"

She reached for the book, but Jack grabbed her hand. "Don't touch it!"

Just then was another flash of lightning with the thunder right on top; the castle seemed to jump. One of the oversized portraits on the wall leapt off, somersaulting straight toward Martha's head. Scott and I both made to block Martha. He pushed her out of the way, while I wedged myself in front of her. The result was that Scott and I banged our noggins together, and I fell onto the floor. The portrait crashed down on top of me, the corner of the heavy frame knocking into my temple.

The room seemed to spin for a moment, then a red haze clouded over my vision.

A bloodcurdling scream filled the air, as darkness descended upon me.

Ten
·················

INT. DINING ROOM DAY

Scott is seated at the dining room table. In front of him is a tea place setting; he grips the teacup as if to drink, but sets it down again. He looks directly into the camera, his handsome face serious and earnest.

SCOTT
(*smiles*) Hello, America. Here I am again. The last time I was in front of this confessional camera was on *For Love or Money*. I poured my heart out about how much I loved Georgia, and today I'm here to plead our case to stay on this investigation. You

see, Georgia would be here herself . . .
(rubs at his shaved head) but some crazy
stuff has been going on in the castle.
*(He glances down at the teacup. When he
looks back up at the camera, his
expression is grim.)* I'm supposed to ask
you to vote for Georgia and me. But the
truth is, I'm not really capable of
conducting an investigation. I can do
research, sure. I can do that with the
best of them . . . but Georgia is the
real investigator. Only . . . *(He closes
his eyes, sucks in a noisy breath through
his teeth.)* She's hurt. She's been hurt
twice here in this place and I'd really
rather have her be safe and sound, than
stay on this show and continue to be
hurt . . . or worse.
(He pauses and looks pained.) That makes me
selfish. Doesn't it? Georgia wants to stay. I
know she does. What's that stupid cliché? If
you love someone, set them free?
*(He glances around the room as if looking
for answers, then fidgets with the teacup
and saucer in front of him.)* Georgia can
figure out who killed Jane Reiner. She can
get justice for Jane. I know it, and you
know it, America. Vote for her. She deserves
your vote.

....

M y eyes fluttered open to Cheryl standing above me. "Again? Really?" she demanded.

"What happened?" I asked. I looked around the room, trying to place myself. We were in the library, the cast and crew were huddled around an open book, some of them were absorbed by it, others were watching me carefully.

It came back me, the Ouija board, the book, the flying portrait. I propped myself up on my elbows, my head pounding.

"How long have I been out?" I asked. I pressed at my temple and found gauze.

"Long enough for Jose to bandage you up. How do you feel?" Cheryl asked.

I mentally assessed myself. My leg seemed to sting more than my head, so I mumbled, "I'm okay. Where's Scott?"

"He was hovering over you like a mother hen. I sent him off to do the voter plea. We're editing footage for tonight, because we have the first round of voting. Eliminations are tomorrow, remember? I can't let the schedule slip." She reached out and helped me to my feet.

"Well, between the Ouija board and the Harry Potter book, or whatever, I'm sure you got enough spook footage for the episode, right?"

Once on my feet, the room seemed to give another twirl. I reached out and grabbed Cheryl's shoulder to steady myself. There was a little twinkle in her eye as she said, "Don't you believe in other worldly messages?"

Before I could answer, she patted my hand. "You need your rest. We're going to stop the formal filming now, serve dinner, and then get whatever we can overnight."

"Food?" Dr. Arch asked, making no bones about the fact that he was eavesdropping on our conversation.

"Yup, the buffet is already set up," Cheryl said.

Dr. Arch laced an arm through mine. "You do need to fuel up. Two injuries in one day. If I didn't know any better, I'd say the spirits are targeting you."

Jack followed us out of the room. "Well, I do know better, and that's exactly what I think."

I ignored them and hobbled down the hallway, my nose leading the way. The fragrant scent of butternut squash soup and toasted bread beckoned. Once inside the dining room, the table was again set buffet-style. This time a large soup tureen was on the right, followed by a few chafing dishes to the left.

Scott was already in the dining room and he rushed to my side, enveloping me in a hug. "Oh, my goodness. Georgia! How's your head?"

I leaned into his embrace and greedily soaked up his attention. "I'm fine," I soothed.

"Hot dish?" Bert asked, excitedly stroking his red beard. "Someone must have complained about the sandwiches!"

"Guilty as charged," Dr. Arch said, grabbing a plate and cutting to the front of the buffet line. "We can't be expected to chase down ghosts on salads and sandwiches!"

"That's right," Jack said, following closely behind him. "We need something that will stick to our ribs." He pulled the top of the chafing dish off to reveal a concoction that must have alarmed him, because he dropped the cover back with a clang and said, "Vegan? Gluten free? How is that supposed to provide us any sustenance?"

Dr. Arch grabbed a ladle and served himself the butternut squash soup. "I wanted to be considerate of the ladies. They're always watching their figures. Karen will love . . . what is it exactly?"

They peered into the dish together, then read the label neatly typed in front of the dish. "Potato and fenugreek curry," Jack said.

Dr. Arch wrinkled his nose. "Let's try the next one."

"Tofu and broccoli stir-fry served with brown rice," Jack whined.

Scott stifled a chuckle.

Dr. Arch moved to the final chafing dish and read, "Grilled Saba banana skewers with jicama and apple salad."

Jack put a hand over his heart and sucked in a breath as if gravely injured. Meanwhile, Bert lumbered past them and piled his plate with everything saying, "Super! Bananas, potatoes, broccoli—this is all brain food."

"Where's the protein?" Dr. Arch complained.

"Red meat?" Scott asked. "I don't think that's vegan."

I grabbed a piece of toast. "It's a good thing we're not hungry," I said.

Dr. Arch sighed. "I'm going to have to have another chat with that producer."

"Good luck," I said, trying not to imagine the crew

stuffing themselves on prime grass-fed beef over at the Indian casino.

The women, Karen, Martha, Jessica, and Ashley, filtered through the buffet line and happily piled their plates with jicama and apple salad.

Father Gabriel patted Dr. Arch's shoulder. "I'm sure we can all find something here that satisfies. Remember Proverb 10:3: 'The Lord will not allow a righteous person to starve.'"

"Speaking of righteous, father," I said. "Can you tell me what you were doing on the third floor this afternoon?"

He turned to me, a look of alarm on his face. "My dear! I was not on the third floor."

Dr. Arch stepped between us and growled, "I told you that already. We weren't there. Maybe that little bump on the head was worse than we thought."

Scott snaked an arm around my waist. "Come on, G. You can't squeeze blood from a turnip."

I let Scott pull me away, but I leveled a gaze at Father Gabriel. "I know Dr. Arch is a liar, but I expected more from you, father."

After eating we roamed back into the main living room where the sleeping bags were laid out in the same sort of arrangement as the night before. As night fell, the cast became a bit subdued. I wondered if they were more upset about the groundskeeper being found dead or the upcoming elimination.

Then I overheard Jessica and Ashley grumbling about the elimination and my suspicions were confirmed.

"Did you know the groundskeeper?" I asked Ashley.

She looked over at me, surprised. "Me? No. Why would I know him?"

"Well, you work here as the paranormal docent. I thought maybe you knew him."

Ashley shook her head. "I haven't worked here long. I barely know anyone."

Scott uncapped the bottle of rum and passed it to Jessica, who eagerly took a sip. I tried to hide my annoyance.

Bert tapped my shoulder. "I have some chocolate left." He wiggled the near-empty white box under my nose. "Do you like dark chocolate? It seems to be the last solid piece."

"Then, I'm in luck," I said, popping the piece into my mouth.

He smiled.

"Bert, what do you feel when you get a premonition?" I asked.

"What do you mean?"

"Well, about the groundskeeper. You said that you had a sense that he'd been drowned. What happens to you when you have that thought?"

He nodded and closed his eyes, taking my question seriously. "It's almost like I visualize it, Georgia, like when you read a book and you see the description, you can see it in your mind's eye. That's the best way that I can describe it. I saw it in my mind's eye."

"Well, did you see how he could have drowned, given that it was an empty pool?" I asked.

He shook his head. "No, no. He didn't drown in the pool. He drowned away from there."

"So you're saying you think somebody killed him and then dropped the body off at the bottom of the pool?"

He nodded.

"That doesn't make any sense though. Why would anyone do that?" I asked.

Bert shrugged. "Perhaps that wasn't their intention. Maybe they were looking for a place to hide the body, and they got interrupted somehow."

A shiver zipped up my spine. I had been out in front of the pool.

Had I interrupted the murderer discarding the body?

I wanted to talk to Becca, see what she remembered, but there was no way to reach her. "Bert, do you have any idea how I can get in touch with my friend?"

His face lit up. "You mean Becca?"

"Yes," I said. "We don't have any phones."

He laughed. "What? You think because I'm psychic I can message her telepathically?"

I reddened. I hadn't thought that intentionally. After all, I barely believed in all this hocus-pocus, but somehow I'd figured he could help me.

Bert stroked his beard thoughtfully. "Maybe you could ask the producer? Tell her it's an emergency."

"Cheryl's not going to let me call her," I said.

"We can always try," he said with a smile.

I pictured him and Becca together for a moment. It was clear he was smitten with her, but could she be interested in dating a psychic who looked like a lumberjack?

"Not we," I corrected.

He looked chagrined.

The best way I knew to get in touch with Becca would be through one of the crew members, somebody who wouldn't mind bending the rules a bit for me. "If they haven't locked us in the room, I'll see what I can do," I said.

I turned to Scott, who was now lying on his sleeping bag with one hand covering his eyes. "I'll be right back," I said.

He let out a soft snore in response.

Everyone else seemed to be settling down to sleep now, too. I crept toward the door of the drawing room and found it unlocked. "I'll see if my luck holds up," I said to Bert.

He nodded. "Let's hope it's the dark chocolate kind of luck and not the fall-through-the-floor kind."

I hesitated. "Do you have a bad feeling right now?"

He shook his head. "No. That was my attempt at humor. Go."

I left the room and wandered through the dark castle. The hallway was so obscure, that I touched the wall as a guide, wishing I'd made nice with Father Gabriel, who had a flashlight. As it was, shadows seemed to dance around me, and for one horrifying moment, I thought I saw a pair of legs, complete with fifties-style cuffed jeans and loafers, jutting from the wall.

My imagination was getting the best of me.

I took a deep breath to calm my racing heart, and reached the little phone kiosk. Suddenly a ringing sounded as if there were a phone call, but the kiosk was empty. No phone. Only the sound of ringing.

I shook it off, and hurried the rest of the way down the hallway, muttering to myself. These strange sights and sounds were either all in my head or some sort of gotcha for Cheryl's hidden cameras.

I reached the main spiral staircase and hobbled down the steps and out of the castle. A cold breeze buffeted my face, chilling and fortifying me at the same time. There was nothing like a California evening breeze after a rain. I glanced up at the night sky illuminated by the three-quarter moon. Orion the hunter and Sirius the dog were visible and for a moment I felt at home.

Down the hill from the castle was a row of modular housing units. Some lights were on in one of the units and I hoped perhaps someone from the crew had stayed back and was in there editing footage or monitoring viewer votes.

On my way, I saw a figure approach. I recognized him as Adam, my cameraman.

He waved hello to me with his flashlight. "What are you doing out, Georgia? Isn't that against the rules?" he asked.

I shrugged. "I don't know if it is or isn't, but I wanted to make a phone call, and that's probably, definitely against the rules."

He laughed. "Who are you going to call? Ghostbusters?"

"Not funny," I said. "What are you doing here? Baby-sitting us?"

He nodded. "Sort of, but only for a little while more. I'm going to join the others at the Indian casino and grab some dinner." He handed me his cell phone. "Go ahead, I won't tell anyone."

I dialed Becca, but when I got her voice mail, I left her a brief message. "Becca, it's G. I'm calling from my cameraman's phone. Wondering if we could have a quick chat. Call me at this number when you get a chance." I disconnected and looked at Adam.

"I'll come let you know if she calls back."

I handed him the phone. "Do you have any idea how the elimination's going?" I asked.

He shrugged. "That's what everyone's all working on. The first episode was incredible. The votes are coming in like crazy. I'm not supposed to say anything, but between you and me, you've got nothing to worry about."

"Is that so?" I asked.

He nodded.

I knew Cheryl had some favorites on the cast and then there were some she wasn't quite fond of. How closely would she stick to audience votes? "Do you think Cheryl's going to ax the priest and the historian no matter what the viewers say?" I asked.

Adam laughed. "No way! She's a by-the-books person. She'll strictly go by what the audience says. She never ever wants to risk the wrath of the viewer."

We giggled together.

"You're right. She wouldn't want that," I said.

"But I get why you asked," Adam said. "She sometimes comes off like she thinks she knows what's best for everyone, sort of like giving you your medicine."

"Right," I agreed.

"Problem is, she's usually right," he said.

Both my head and my leg ached, and I wondered if Cheryl had been right about everything. I was awfully accident prone these days. "Don't tell anyone I was out here," I said.

"Don't worry," he said. "Your secret's safe with me."

As I turned to go, a thought struck me. I stopped and faced him again. "Hey, Adam, do you know who put the voltmeter at the bottom of the pool?"

"Sure," he said. "That was Brendan."

"Do you know if he saw anything? Did the police question him?"

"Yeah, they questioned him for a long time, but I don't think he saw anything."

"Do you know where he is?" I asked.

"He should be at the casino already, stuffing his face with the all-you-can-eat lobster."

My stomach rumbled and Adam looked alarmed. He glanced over his shoulder and flashed his light over toward the bushes. "Did you hear that?"

"That was my stomach," I confessed.

He waved a hand at me. "No, no. Some noise from the bushes."

"Trust me. It was my stomach. You should see the vegan wonderment buffet Cheryl put out for us."

Adam returned his attention to me, unconvinced. "I don't know. This place gives me the creeps. Ever since we found that poor guy at the bottom of the pool, I've been looking over my shoulder constantly."

"I'd like to talk to Brendan. Can you get him a message from me?" I asked.

"Sure," he said. "No problem. I'll let him know to come find you in the morning." Just then, Adam's phone rang and he looked at the caller ID. "I think this is probably for you."

He handed me the phone and I recognized Becca's number. As soon as I picked up, she said, "Georgia! Are you all right?"

"Yes, yes. I'm fine."

"Thank goodness!" Her voice came out in a rush and I knew her so well I suspected her hand was over her heart, trying to calm herself. "Cheryl ended the first episode with you falling through the floor! Your dad and I have been worried sick. I didn't have a way to reach you. We called Cheryl, but she hasn't called us back yet."

"I'm fine," I soothed. "Dr. Arch stitched me up."

"The archaeologist?" she screeched.

I laughed. "Turns out he is a podiatrist. It's gotta be a nickname, right? Get it, a foot doctor named Arch."

"Hmm." Becca harrumphed. "Sounds like Hollywood humor. I'm sure a roomful of creatives thought themselves very clever to come up with that." Her voice dropped an octave for her rendition of a half-witted screenwriter. "A foot doctor playing an archaeologist on TV; let's call him Dr. Arch. Ha-ha."

I snickered. "I see you miss the behind-the-scenes action."

She laughed despite herself. "You bet."

"Hey, I wanted to ask you something though. Last night, before you and Dad left for the farm—"

"Yeah?"

"Did you notice anything strange when we were chatting at the pool?" I asked.

"Strange? Like what?"

It suddenly struck me that Becca didn't know about the groundskeeper. I brought her up to speed as quickly as I could while Adam listened in. Occasionally, he'd flash his light into the bushes. I absently wondered if he'd been having nightmares since we'd found the body.

"A body?" Becca howled. "No wonder Cheryl hasn't returned our call."

"What do you mean?" I asked.

"Seems likes she was avoiding us today. You have her running around in circles, right?"

"I don't know about that. Seems more like she's the one running us ragged. Anyway, last night when we were talking in front of the pool. Did you see or hear anything?"

"No," Becca said.

"I ran into Dr. Arch after you left. Like he was hovering around waiting for you to go."

Becca was silent for a moment, then said. "So what

does that mean? He probably has the hots for you. Was he waiting for me to leave so he could talk to you or something?"

"Or something."

"Just because he was hanging around waiting for you doesn't mean he killed the poor groundskeeper, G."

"I know."

Then there was the incident on the third floor.

Where he denied even being up there. But I didn't want to drag Becca through all my suppositions, especially not in front of Adam.

"You said Dr. Arch is probably not his real name," I said.

"Of course it isn't," she said.

"It's like what? A stage name or something?"

"Yes," she replied patiently, as if I were a two-year-old, so naive in terms of Hollywood glam.

Who was the real Dr. Arch and what were his ties to the Golden Castle?

"What's his real name?" I asked.

"I don't know. I didn't do the casting on this one. That was Cheryl."

"Can you find out for me?" I asked.

At this question, Adam stuck his fingers in his ears and began to sing, "La la la."

Becca sighed. "I can't give you inside information. That's cheating!"

"It's not cheating," I insisted.

Adam sang louder.

"How is it cheating?" I asked them both. "I'm not asking for information about Jane Reiner. Just about another contestant!"

Before Becca could reply, Adam snatched the phone out of my hand. "You aren't even supposed to be using the phone! If Cheryl finds out, I could be fired." Into the phone, he said, "Ignore her. She's had a bump on the head."

Through the phone, I heard Becca's voice. "I thought she hurt her leg?"

Adam snorted. "Long story. Stay tuned for tomorrow's episode. We saved the little doozy for our opening." He hung up the phone and turned toward me. "If your string of bad luck continues, I might have to ask for a reassignment."

"Thanks a lot, Adam," I said.

He walked away from me, his flashlight lighting the way back to the mobile housing units. Over his shoulder, he called, "Hey, all I'm saying is I don't want to film your death."

Eleven

....

had a fitful night. Every time I moved in my sleep, stabbing pains from my leg woke me. The rest of the group
seemed to have no troubles snoring away, but soon enough
everyone awoke to the sound of footsteps down the
hallway.

It was still early, but since I'd been awake for hours, I
was the first to scramble out of my sleeping bag. My
knees almost buckled under my weight. My back was
stiff from the hard wood floor and from twisting up in
the sleeping bag trying to avoid lying on my right leg.

Kyle along with some other crew members roused the
group. This morning, Kyle was decked out in skintight
houndstooth pants paired with a black T-shirt. The outfit
was completed by a red scarf and matching red cowboy
boots.

"Up and at 'em, sunshines. We need to get into hair and makeup immediately," he shouted, clapping his hands for effect.

Dr. Arch startled out of his sleeping bag. "Makeup? What about breakfast?"

"Continental style in the other room. Now get up! Up, up, up! With all yesterday's mishaps, we're frightfully close to running behind schedule," Kyle said.

Some crewmembers began clearing the room, practically rolling up Scott's sleeping bag with him still inside it.

Kyle closed the distance between us and pulled me off to the side. "Georgia. You need to see Cheryl in her office. Immediately."

A sick feeling hit me in my gut. Was this about last night?

Had she found out about my phone call to Becca?

"Where's her office?" I asked.

"She's camped out in one of the manufactured homes. I can walk you down," he said.

He directed me toward the door. "Wait," I said. "At least let me get my shoes on!"

I slipped into my pair of hiking boots and leaned into Scott, who was still rubbing the sleep out of his eyes.

"I'll be right back," I said to Scott.

He nodded. "I'll go save a cup of coffee and a croissant from the buffet for you. Chocolate if they have it."

My heart warmed. He remembered chocolate croissants were my favorite.

Kyle and I left the room and slipped out into the drafty

hallway. Kyle flung his arms wide, his red scarf draping behind him, cape-like, as we walked. "I absolutely love this place! Don't you?"

"Are you mad? This place has the ultimate creep factor going on."

Kyle shook his head. "No. It just needs attention. I think after the show is done, I might volunteer to be on the renovation committee."

I stared at him, wide-eyed. "I bet you'd be great at that. You have a great eye for style. Decor must be along the same lines, right?"

"There has to be a lot of repairs first, before decor, though. I've been chatting with Gertrude." He winked at me. "I think she has a soft spot for me."

I giggled. "Repair work? What? Like you're a hulking construction worker now?"

Kyle laughed. "Don't knock it. I look hot dressed up like a construction guy."

While Kyle was about as good-looking as a man could be, he did drift toward the pretty side of handsome. And if his colorful style wasn't a dead giveaway that he was about as far away from construction experience as one could get, his delicate slim manicured fingers gave him away.

"You'd be the prettiest construction man on the crew. I'm sure," I teased.

We walked outside of the castle and he shielded his eyes from the sun. "Thank you, G. I think you're pretty, too."

I smiled at him. "Seriously, though. Now that I have you alone. What does Cheryl want?"

He shrugged his shoulders. "I don't know. She didn't tell me. Just said to get you."

We continued down the gravel path toward the mobile houses, where I'd been last night with Adam. "Do you know Brendan?" I asked.

"Sure," Kyle said. "'Course. This is a small crew, believe it or not."

"I heard he put the voltmeter down in the pool yesterday, before I found the body. I wanted to speak to him—"

Kyle held up a hand. "Whoa! Wait a minute. You don't think Brendan had anything to do with that guy's death, do you?"

"Well, no. But I mean, I don't know him—"

"Besides," Kyle said, interrupting me again. "Wasn't it an accident? The man fell in and died, right?"

"We don't know that yet."

"That's what Gertrude told me," Kyle said.

I imagined that for the historical society that would be the best story to circulate. An accident. Nothing unseemly going on. Just an accident.

Kyle seemed to sense my disbelief because he lunged at me, clutching my arm in a dramatic fashion. "OMG! Girl! What do you think? You think Brendan killed that poor man?" He sucked in his breath and thumped his free hand over his chest. "I never did trust him, you know? He's got those weasel eyes."

I pulled my arm free from his clutch. "Weasel eyes don't mean—"

"And there was the fight!"

"What fight?" I asked.

"I heard Brendan and the groundskeeper had a fight. Brendan trampled some roses when he was hiding stuff for the scavenger hunt. The groundskeeper got all over him."

Was that enough for murder?

Maybe the argument had escalated?

"When did they argue?" I asked.

"The night before you found him dead," Kyle said. He looked at me meaningfully, as if he was convinced we'd just uncovered a killer in our midst.

Could he be right?

With a flap of his scarf, Kyle left me at the door of Cheryl's office. I knocked and waited for her to call, "Come in!"

When I entered, I was surprised to find that she wasn't alone. Next to her, seated at her makeshift desk was a lean, tan gentlemen dressed in a suit. On Cheryl's desk was a stack of manila folders and a MacBook Pro laptop that was closed. The room was small, and had a claustrophobic feel. All the windows were painted shut and the walls were cluttered with old Indian sand art.

Cheryl stood. Her blond hair was pinned back in a loose bun, and she was dressed in a cream-colored business suit that hugged her curves like a drowning child hanging on to a lifeboat. "Georgia. Thank you for coming so quickly. This is Mr. Martin. He's an attorney with RTV Studios."

My throat went dry. An attorney? Was he to inform me that I'd broken the rules and would therefore be kicked off the show?

Mr. Martin stood and thrust a hand in my direction. I shook it, suddenly feeling wildly underdressed and unprepared for this meeting.

He flashed an oozing Hollywood smile. Uneasiness stirred inside me. If I was about to get kicked off the show, why was he bothering with the charm?

"Ms. Thornton, I understand you had a very rough day yesterday," he said.

I froze. Did he know about the groundskeeper? No. He was an attorney for the TV studios, not a criminal attorney. I said nothing.

He stroked the bridge of his nose. "Your leg was injured. Your head . . ."

I pressed my lips together and glanced at Cheryl, who lowered her eyes.

"I understand you even needed stitches," Mr. Martin continued.

At the mention of my wound, my leg burned and throbbed, as if it were rearing its head when we discussed it. I rubbed at it absently, hoping to soothe it.

Mr. Martin picked up a folder off Cheryl's desk and tapped it against his palm. "Ms. Thornton, had you been advised not to go to the third floor?"

I looked around the office and saw for the first time a hidden camera. Why would Cheryl have a camera in her office? I turned to her. "What's this about?"

"We need to make sure you aren't going to sue RTV Studios, Georgia. I'm sorry," Cheryl said.

"Sue?" I asked. I racked my brain. Hadn't we all signed waivers before we began filming? I was sure I'd signed a hold-harmless about death and dismemberment. "You need me to sign another waiver or something?"

Mr. Martin flashed me his lawyer smile. "Well, yes, Georgia." He flipped open the folder and laid it out across the desk. "If you wouldn't mind."

I glanced at Cheryl. "How is this waiver different than the other one?" I asked. "I believe we all signed—"

"You received medical care from someone in the cast. We didn't sanction that," Mr. Martin explained. "I need you to confirm that it was your choice to receive that care. Should you develop, say, an infection or . . ." His dark eyes searched the ceiling as if the answer were up there along with the yellowing, chipped paint. After a moment, he concluded with "worse."

Cheryl shifted uncomfortably. "Well, Dr. Arch is a medical doctor," she said, her voice turning shrill. "Jose is only an EMT."

Mr. Martin nodded reassuringly at her. "No one is questioning your judgment. You did the best you could under the circumstances." He put a hand on my shoulder. "I'm sure everything will be fine, but you understand, Georgia. We just need your signature." He pointed to the bottom of the sheet. "Here." He turned the page. "Here." He turned another page. "And here. And if you wouldn't mind initialing at the bottom of every page."

I stared at the file. It was about thirty pages long. "Well, can I read it?" I asked.

"Certainly, certainly," Mr. Martin lulled, showing me his even, square white teeth. He turned to Cheryl and indicated the door.

Cheryl nodded. "Right. Take your time, Georgia. Except hurry. We need to get on with our filming."

They left the mobile office, the flimsy door clunking closed. I quickly scanned the file. It looked fairly boiler-plate. I really had no problem signing it. I'd been of sound mind accepting Dr. Arch's care. There was a section explaining that the waiver did not include my acquiescing my rights to sue Dr. Arch should I lose my leg.

Egads!

Was that really possible? Lose a leg from stitches? Well, with an infection anything was possible. But even though the wound burned, I doubted I had an infection. I turned my back toward the hidden camera, blocking the view to ensure my privacy, then lowered my pants and checked the wound. There was a bit of clear seepage from it, which was normal. But I was relieved to see there were no angry red tentacles radiating from it. So far, I was infection free. I yanked up my pants and signed the paper-work. As I picked up the file to return it to Mr. Martin, the file beneath it became visible.

Across the top of the file, in red block print was *CON-FIDENTIAL: THE TRUTH ABOUT THE MURDER OF JANE REINER.*

I hesitated. My breath rushed out of my lungs as if I'd just finished a sprint.

Did Cheryl have the answer to the unsolved murder?

My fingers hovered above the file, itching to open it.

Then the thought struck me. The cameras!

Was this a trap?

Twelve

....

I stepped out of the dark office into the brightness of the day. Despite the early hour, the day was heating up and Cheryl and Mr. Martin were standing under the shade of a large oak tree.

I walked over to them and handed Mr. Martin the file. "Here you are," I said. "All signed and initialed."

He nodded and flipped through the file quickly. "I appreciate your cooperation." He glanced at his gold wristwatch. "If I want to catch my flight, I better head out."

Cheryl looked sour. No doubt she was probably wishing she could head back to L.A. with him.

Mr. Martin said good-bye to us, then turned on the heel of his designer shoe and strolled back up the gravel path toward the parking lot of the castle.

We watched him walk away for a moment, and when

I was sure he was out of earshot, said, "I'm sorry, if I got you in trouble."

Cheryl waved a hand dismissing me. "Pfft. I know you're not going to sue, but that awful woman, Gertrude, called corporate and raised a stink. They dispatched Martin out in short order."

"She called them about what? My injury?"

Cheryl laughed. "Oh, heck no. She doesn't care about your leg. It was a complaint about the destruction to the castle."

"Ugh." I sighed. "The third floor?"

Cheryl nodded. "Yup. That woman is driving me crazy. She's trying to get us out of here as soon as possible. I don't know what it's to her. The masquerade fundraising ball isn't for another few weeks. We can get a construction crew to come in here and repair the third floor by then," she said.

Guilt flooded me. I was responsible for the damage to the third floor, but certainly I didn't have any money to pay for repairs.

Would the studio sue me?

"Maybe I should have Mr. Martin prepare a hold-harmless for me," I said.

Cheryl smiled. "Ha! Now that's an idea. I should sue you for damages, huh?"

I must have paled because Cheryl patted my arm. "Just kidding. The network made a ton of money last night. The footage of you falling through the floor is golden." Suddenly, she looked in the direction of the parking lot and her face grew serious.

"What is it?" I asked, following her line of vision.

"The police," she said, as my eyes landed on a cruiser parked in the lot. "Urgh," she grumbled. "What is it now?"

Excitement stirred inside me, and despite my wound, I hustled back up the hill toward the cruiser. "News!" I said.

Cheryl hurried behind me, but her impractical high heels proved to slow her down worse than my bum leg. "Let me handle this, Georgia!" she yelled after me.

"No way," I called. "This is right up my alley. There must be some development."

"I need you to get into hair and makeup! I can't risk the show," Cheryl screeched. She clicked and clacked behind me, and reached out to grab me, but I hobbled quicker, grateful for my hiking boots.

"Stop! Georgia!" she hollered.

We must have made a sight, and I absently wondered where the cameras might be. Although Cheryl would never air her image, especially if she happened to look foolish.

She made a last ditch effort to lunge at me, but she was too slow. I was already cresting the hill to the parking lot. I waved at the officer from the other day, as he stepped out of his car. He turned to watch the taillights of Mr. Martin's black rental car as it exited the parking lot.

I limped up to him. "Hello, officer. What's going on? Have you found something?" I asked.

He looked grim, but said nothing as Cheryl closed the distance on us. She waved both hands in the air in an effort to make us wait for her before discussing anything. Then she carefully tucked behind her ear a strand of blond hair that had freed itself during her mad dash.

"Officer! Officer Holtz. Can I help you?" she asked, stepping in front of me.

I sidestepped her, but she pushed at my waist, clearly indicating that I should hightail it back into the castle.

I ignored her and seemingly the officer did, too, because he said, "Well, it wasn't an accident. The autopsy reports are in. It looks like the groundskeeper was definitely murdered."

Cheryl sucked in a noisy breath. "Murdered? No, no. It must have been an accident—"

"How can you be so sure?" I asked him.

"There was water in his lungs. He drowned, and there was no water at the bottom of the pool, so he was drowned off-location and was discarded in the pool."

I shuddered. This seemed to match what Bert had told me. But how could Bert have known? I really had my doubts about Bert being psychic.

Could he be the murderer?

But if he was, then why would he alert us to the cause of death?

I turned to the officer. "Have you spoken with a crew member named Brendan?"

Officer Holtz nodded. "I did. He was the one that left the contraption in the pool, right?"

"The voltmeter. Yes," Cheryl said.

The officer glanced around the parking lot as if looking

for a clue. "Right. Yeah. He left that thing in the bottom of the pool before the groundskeeper was in there apparently. He said that he hadn't seen anything. Still, he was very helpful. Helped us nail down the time of death."

Something wasn't quite right. I wanted to talk to Brendan myself, but in the meantime, I asked the police officer, "Have you spoken with Kyle?"

"Who's Kyle?" he asked, turning to Cheryl.

"He's my lead hair and makeup person." She frowned at me. "What does Kyle have to do with any of this?"

I relayed to them what Kyle told me about overhearing Brendan and the groundskeeper arguing. The officer pulled out a notebook from his pocket and made a note. A strange sensation filled me as I thought about Kyle.

How quickly he'd thrown Brendan under the bus.

Was he hiding something?

After all, he was the one who had sent me up to the third floor for makeup. Could he deliberately be pointing a finger at Brendan in order to have us focused in the wrong direction?

"Do you have any information on the groundskeeper?" I asked the police officer.

"What do you mean?" he asked.

"Well, on his history, how long he worked here, that sort of thing."

The officer frowned. "Look. I know you may have worked for SFPD in the past, but I'm handling this investigation."

Cheryl beamed. "Yes, you are! And we will leave you

to it!" She slipped her arm through mine. "Come on, Miss G. Let's get you into hair—"

I wiggled out of her grip. "Where did he work before here?" I wondered out loud.

The officer squinted at me, "Oh, he's worked here for the last twenty years."

He turned to Cheryl. "I'm going to need to take statements from your cast."

Cheryl looked as if she'd swallowed a lemon. "But we're already behind schedule! I have to film an episode that airs live tonight."

The officer glared at her. "Lady, this is a murder investigation."

"I understand," Cheryl said, sounding contrite.

The officer nodded. "I need a list of the cast and crew. The one you promised me yesterday. I'd like to speak with them one-on-one. I'll try to be brief. Hopefully that won't impact your schedule too much."

After I left Cheryl and the police officer, I was startled to see Scott sitting on the front porch of the castle chatting with Father Gabriel. Scott was dressed in a tan coverall suit and Father Gabriel had on his traditional black cassock.

In the distance, I waved, but upon seeing me Father Gabriel stood. He gave Scott a blessing, then they hugged. Father Gabriel left the porch to go back inside the castle before I could reach them.

I climbed the rickety wooden steps of the porch to where Scott had settled back down. Next to him was a white paper cup and small plate with a croissant on top.

"Hi there!" I said awkwardly. "Nice outfit," I remarked.

He smiled warmly at me. "My stylist is an idiot. I think he's convinced this makes me look like a ghost hunter."

"Then he should have Jack wear it!"

Scott laughed. "Jack refused. So I guess that makes me the idiot. He handed me the plate and cup. "Got your favorite, but I'm afraid it's probably cold by now."

I took it from him and placed both items on the step next to me. "Thank you." I nodded to the door where Father Gabriel had just disappeared. "What was that about?" I asked.

Scott looked at me sheepishly.

"We were just having a nice chat," Scott said.

I wondered if I had interrupted some sort of confession. "I'm sorry, I didn't mean to interrupt." I sipped my cold coffee, hoping he'd share a little about his conversation with Father Gabriel.

Instead, Scott said, "No problem. How's your head? Your leg?"

"My head's fine. My leg hurts, but it's getting better." I took a bite out of the croissant, suddenly realizing how hungry I was. I finished it in three bites. "Cheryl made me sign a waiver, promise not to sue," I said.

He laughed. "I thought we'd already done that."

"Her fancy Hollywood attorney wanted the extra insurance." I fidgeted next to him, running a finger along the wood grain of the steps. I wanted to tell him about the officer and the autopsy findings, but it seemed like he was biding his time to tell me something. My stomach churned at the thought, the croissant I'd just gobbled twisting my belly into a pretzel.

Please, God, not another chat about his lack of feelings for me.

A splinter jammed into my finger and I recoiled. "Ouch!"

He took my hand in his. "Georgia! You need to be more careful. One of these days, something bigger is going to bite and it won't be easy to recover." He deftly plucked the splinter from my finger.

We were silent for a moment and then I brought him up to speed on the autopsy report. He listened quietly. When I finished, he said nothing, only stared out in the distance at the rolling hills.

I asked, "Anything you want to talk about?"

He shrugged. "Did you know that Father Gabriel attended this reform school when he was a boy?"

"He did?" I asked.

Scott nodded. "Yeah. He said he had a real sketchy past, used to steal and do drugs."

"Wow," I said.

"Yup. Life takes some funny roads, right? Reform school student turns priest. I guess that's real reform."

"Was he here at the time that Jane was murdered?"

Scott shrugged. "He didn't want to tell me."

An uncomfortable sensation squirmed through my belly. The kind of stirring I always felt when my body knew I was onto something before my brain caught up. "I bet he was," I said. "I bet he knows Jane. It would be just like Cheryl to cast someone who knew her, don't you think?"

"Possibly," Scott said, rubbing at the back of his shaved head. "He did seem very hush-hush about it."

I nodded.

"You know the other thing he told me?" he asked.

"What's that?" I asked.

"He said the groundskeeper was also here as a boy. They were friends."

Alarm bells went off in my head. Well, that was quite a coincidence. The groundskeeper had attended the reform school as a boy and so had Father Gabriel?

I jumped up. "We have to talk to him," I said.

Scott looked offended. "I just did! He told me all that in confidence. I don't think he wanted the rest of the cast to know."

"But that was before we knew the autopsy results."

Scott nodded reluctantly. "Right." He stood. "We can find him inside. Let's go."

Scott pulled open the heavy front door of the castle and I followed him inside. Harris, our ever-fearless host, appeared out of nowhere. "What are you doing here?" he said. "It's time to film the next episode. We have an elimination to take care of."

"Can it wait a moment—"

"What? Are you crazy?" Harris snapped. "Broom Hilda waits for no one!"

He meant Cheryl, and I had to giggle at the reference. Broom Hilda was the nickname I'd given her on the first show I'd been on. I shuddered to think that the name had gotten traction. If she knew it was me who had invented it, she was liable to make things even rougher for me.

Harris ushered us inside, muttering under his breath, "Not my job! Corralling the cast! I have to call my agent."

Thirteen

....

was pushed into Kyle's capable arms. He'd laid out a pair of burgundy capri pants paired with a low-cut black tank top for me. He made short order of curling my hair and applying a quick makeup job.

"The others are waiting for you," he said. "What took so long with Cheryl?"

I bit my lip. It wasn't my place to discuss the autopsy findings with Kyle. Anyway, I figured he'd probably already told me what he knew on that topic. There was something else, however, that I could ask him.

"Kyle. When I was in Cheryl's office, I saw a file—"

Kyle took in a sharp intake of breath and his eyes widened.

"What's in the file, Kyle? Do you all already know who killed Jane Reiner?"

Kyle shook his head in a very unconvincing manner. "I don't know what you're talking about," he shrieked.

"Yes, you do! Otherwise, you wouldn't be acting all panicky like that!"

Kyle made an exaggerated show of interest in the array of eye shadows on his makeup palette. "I think we'll go with the brown and gold."

I growled at him, the sound resounding from deep within my throat.

"Down, girl," he said.

"I'm going to find out soon enough and I know who's on my side and who's not," I threatened.

Kyle, now focused on his element, seemed unmoved as he dipped his brush across the brown shadow powder. "Oh, I'm on your side all right. Otherwise, you'd be wearing a canary yellow top that I know for a fact pales you out and would make you look nasty." He graced me with a tight smirk before saying, "Close your eyes, Georgia, and trust me."

Within a few minutes the cast was lined up in front of Harris. Standing next to Scott were Ashley and Jessica, looking ridiculously cute in matching teal pantsuits. Jack, the ghost hunter, was decked out in a Sherlock Holmes–looking outfit, complete with a tweed jacket and an unlit smoking pipe. His partner, Bert, the psychic wore all white, contrasting Father Gabriel's black cassock. Martha, the historian, wore a smart A-line skirt and peach-colored silk blouse, and Dr. Arch and his partner, Karen, were outfitted in jeans and blazers.

On Cheryl's cue, Harris pressed his shoulders back, put on his host expression, and boomed in his over-the-top voice, "Hello, America! And welcome back to *Cold Case in the Castle*! Where we're committed to solving the brutal and disturbing murder of Jane Reiner, the lovely, innocent youth working as a librarian in training, here"—he waved his hands all around him in a dramatic fashion—"on the premises of this reform school."

"As you know." He pointed a finger at the camera. "Last night we asked you to vote, dear viewers, and vote you did!" He pressed a hand over his heart. "We were overwhelmed by your support, flooding the phone lines. We heard you loud and clear!"

As Harris droned on, I thought about the file in Cheryl's office.

Could it be true that the production already knew the identity of the killer?

Harris looked out at the cast and the cameras slowly panned us.

"Cut!" yelled Cheryl. "Georgia, you're supposed to look concerned now. You might be voted off!"

I shrugged. "Don't I look concerned?"

"You look like you want to murder Harris," Cheryl retorted. "Now, come on. Game face. Daylight's burning."

"Jack, Bert!" Harris called out. The camera zoomed in close on their faces. "America has spoken!"

Jack looked disappointed and Bert pressed a hand to his temple.

Ha! Psychic. Well, he hadn't seen that one coming!

"They would like you to continue on the show!" Harris said.

A rush of air escaped Jack, and he appeared visibly relieved. Bert, on the other hand, nodded as if that was the outcome he'd expected all along. His hand didn't drop from his temple, though, and that left me wondering.

"Jessica, Ashley!" Harris called out. The girls clutched hands. "You are safe from elimination."

They hugged excitedly, and then as if on cue, the four safe players looked over worriedly at the rest of us.

For a moment I thought back to Adam last night. He'd said I was safe.

Was I really?

Anxiety rippled through my chest as Harris called out, "Dr. Arch, Karen Kenley! The viewers have spoken—"

Suddenly a dark shadow crossed over Harris's face.

Goose bumps rose on my arms.

"Cut," Cheryl cried out. "What's going on with our lighting?"

One of the techs standing at the main spotlight checked the cord. "Nothing," he said. "Everything is working fine."

"Then why is there a big shadow on Harris's face?" Cheryl asked, her voice full of sarcasm.

Harris looked alarmed. "A shadow?"

"It's a presence," Father Gabriel announced.

Jack stepped closer, his voltmeter at the ready.

Harris jumped back from him. "Don't zap me with that thing, you idiot!"

147

Diana Orgain

Bert clutched at his temple with two hands and shook his head back and forth.

"Not again," Martha wailed. "Let's get on with it! Please tell me we're the ones voted off. Gabriel, did you pray for that like I asked you?"

"All right, everyone, calm down," Cheryl said. "Harris, move back into the light."

When Harris did, the shadow was gone, but the goose bumps on my arm remained.

Harris, like the professional he was, picked up right where he left off. "Dr. Arch, Karen Kenley! Your fans from *Hunting Bones* called in droves. They are confident you can help solve the mystery of Jane Reiner. You are safe from elimination."

Harris drew a breath. "Scott and Georgia."

Scott grabbed my hand, and squeezed my fingers.

Harris continued, "Father Gabriel and Martha. One team will be leaving the castle immediately."

Harris continued to talk as my mind whirled. I'd wanted to speak with Father Gabriel and if we were eliminated now or his team was, my chance would be lost.

"Scott, Georgia," Harris said. "You are safe from elimination." He bowed his head. "Father Gabriel, Martha. I'm sorry. The viewers have spoken, and they've voted for you *not* to continue on the journey of solving the mystery of Jane Reiner."

Father Gabriel looked crestfallen, but Martha clapped her hands together. "Thank goodness. Our prayers have been answered, Gabriel! Let's get out of this godforsaken place."

"Wait!" I screamed out. "I need time with Father Gabriel. He can't be eliminated so quickly."

But Harris ignored me, saying, "Father Gabriel, Martha, please say your good-byes." The cameras panned around the cast while Father Gabriel and Martha hugged each of us.

When it was my turn to hug Father Gabriel, I whispered into his ear, "We need to talk."

He looked at me, and I saw something in his eyes. Was it fear? "Of course, Georgia, of course. Anytime. I'm not leaving right away." He glanced away from me, toward the windows. "I have a few things I need to square up before I go. I'll be in the garden later if you want to meet with me."

"Yes, father, please," I said urgently.

Father Gabriel and Martha were ushered out of the room, and then Harris announced the next challenge. "Now, my dear contestants," he said. "As usual, we have another challenge that will help you solve the mystery. Each clue will give you access to certain parts of the castle that have been previously closed off to you, like the kitchen where the body of Jane Reiner was recovered, and the portion of the library where she worked."

The cast made excited little noises.

Harris pulled out a red envelope from his breast-side pocket and said, "The game will be played *Jeopardy*-style. I'll give you answers and you tell me the questions."

We all nodded our understanding.

"Nineteen twenty-four," Harris called out.

We all looked at each other and then semi-expectantly at Ashley, the paranormal docent. Surely she would know the answer. After all, she worked at the castle as a tour guide.

She bit her lip and shrugged her shoulders.

"Maybe the castle was built that year," Scott said to me.

"I need the answer in the form of a question," Harris said.

"What year was the castle built?" Dr. Arch shouted out, flashing a "take that" look in Scott's direction.

"Exactly!" Harris said, excitedly. "You and your partner have gained access to the basement downstairs, where some of the boys who attended the reform school had their dormitories!"

Karen clutched at Dr. Arch's arm and batted her long false eyelashes at him. "You always come through!"

"Lanny McMillian," Harris called out.

"Who is the best running back of all time?" Ashley asked.

I frowned at her.

She works at the castle. How can she not know the answer?

"Who is the most famous inmate of Golden Castle Reform School?" I guessed.

"Correct!" Harris said. "Georgia, you and Scott will now have access to the kitchen, where the body of Jane Reiner was discovered."

Scott high-fived me, then all of a sudden, Bert started moaning. "My head, my head!" he screamed out, pressing his fingers to his forehead.

Bert grabbed at me. "Georgia, Georgia."

"What is it?" I asked, my patience wearing thin.

"I see a black aura around you,"

"Black aura? What the heck does that mean?" Scott asked, clutching at my wrist and pulling me away from Bert.

"Extreme danger," Bert announced. "You must call your father instantly."

"My father?" Nervous energy shot through me, almost making me choke.

Cheryl called out "Cut!" to the crew, which flocked around us. "What are you saying?" she asked Bert.

"Gordon. I think Gordon's in extreme danger," he said.

Cheryl flashed me a look. "Everyone, take five minutes," she said, then she pulled out her cell phone and dialed my father's number.

Fourteen

....

When my father didn't answer his phone, I tried to calm Cheryl down.

"Let's try Becca," I insisted. "They have to be together, or at least she may know where he is. Remember there's a lot of areas of the farm that are out of range of his cell service."

After several futile attempts, I asked, "Why are we getting all panicked? We don't know anything for sure yet."

She waved me off. "The psychic said Gordon's in trouble. That's enough for me."

"Well what do you want to do?" I said.

"Let's go to Cottonwood right away," she said.

"But, it's an hour's drive," I said. "What about your production schedule and all?"

Cheryl's panic was beginning to rub off on me, but I was determined to fight for my sanity. After all, chances were Dad and Becca just couldn't get to the phone at the moment. If we were patient and waited, the logical part of my brain told me, they would surface momentarily.

"It doesn't matter. We'll put production on hold."

"On hold?" I asked, incredulous.

Cheryl suddenly looked like a doe caught in the headlights. "You're right! I can't put the thing on hold. Kyle!" she screamed.

He materialized next to us as if out of thin air.

"Yes, Broom Hilda?"

"Don't call me that!" Cheryl said through gritted teeth. "I need you to keep filming while I'm gone. Get some confessionals and footage in my office."

Kyle tilted his head in a coquettish fashion. "Am I in charge while you're gone?" he asked.

Cheryl looked defeated momentarily, then squared her shoulders. "Okay, you can be in charge," she pointed a finger in his face, "but no margarita machines!"

Kyle gave her a mock salute.

Cheryl shouted some instructions over to Adam. "Keep Kyle in line!"

We raced over to the parking lot where Cheryl's Jeep was parked.

Scott ran up to us. "Not without me, you don't," he said, climbing in. "What's going on?"

"Nothing really," I said. "At least I hope not. We just can't reach Dad or Becca."

"I hope it's nothing serious," Cheryl said, putting the pedal to the metal.

She took the turn so hard that Scott slid from behind the passenger side to behind the driver side. "Maybe I should drive," he said.

"Don't be ridiculous," Cheryl said. "There's nothing wrong with my driving. Just put your seat belt on and shut your mouth. I can't stand backseat drivers." Then, she took a turn that nearly careened us off the road into a ditch.

"Cheryl," I said. "You've got to calm down. We don't know anything yet!"

"You're right. You're right," she said. She eased up on the gas a bit, and put us into the legal speeding zone. While Cheryl drove, Scott and I attempted to reach my father and Becca by phone again.

"It's not unusual for them not to answer," I said. "They're busy with harvest. It's not like they're sitting around waiting for their phones to ring."

Cheryl grunted. "Well, he always seems to answer the phone when I call." When I didn't respond, she added, "On the first ring. He usually answers on the first ring."

I laughed. Cheryl and my father had a very cute budding romance, and it was probably true. Anytime he saw her phone number come across the screen, he dove for the phone.

"Well, they could be outside running the equipment. It's noisy," I justified, although the pit in my stomach was growing.

Why weren't they answering their phones?

Could a psychic really be right about trouble for my dad?

Was Bert even psychic?

I envisioned different scenarios of how we'd find them. At the house maybe the phones were being charged while they were having lunch. Or . . . they were taking a nap . . . or a shower . . . or any number of possibilities, really.

There had to be a logical solution.

"Is there a local police station we can call?" Cheryl asked. "Somebody who's closer to check in on them?"

I shook my head. "The county sheriff's department is miles out. We'll get there faster, but I can call the neighbors." I dialed our neighbor Mrs. Wassermann and waited. Finally, her voice mail picked up. She had her full agenda on there. Today was the day that she played bridge with her friends, after which she was heading over to the Mucky Duck for dinner. So, needless to say, she wasn't around to check on my dad.

After calling several of the other neighbors, I was finally able to reach Mr. Hornsby. He promised to drive over to the farm and see how my dad was.

INT. CHERYL'S OFFICE DAY

The office is empty. Kyle marches in followed by Dr. Arch.

Diana Orgain

KYLE

(*smiles*) Thank you for your cooperation,
doctor. I'm sure you understand that this is
all a matter of formality. (*He riffles
through Cheryl's desk.*) Now, where is it?
That woman! She never files anything
properly. (*He pulls out his cell phone.*) Ack.
No service. (*He pats Dr. Arch on the arm.*)
I'll be right back. Don't touch a thing.
She'll cook my goose if I fowl this up!
(*Kyle leaves the office. Dr. Arch is alone.
He looks down at the desk and sees a folder.
Across the top of the file, in red block
print reads,* CONFIDENTIAL: THE TRUTH ABOUT
THE MURDER OF JANE REINER.*)*
(*Dr. Arch drops the file as if stung, then
after a moment, he glances out the window
looking for Kyle. When he sees no imminent
threat of interruption, he picks up the
folder and opens it. His face pales and his
jaw drops as he reads the first page.*)

When we arrived at my father's farmhouse, Mr.
Hornsby was the only one we found. He was sitting
in his pickup out front. I waved heartily to him. He got
out of the pickup immediately and embraced me.

"Georgia, it's been so long since I've seen you!" he
said. "And now you're a verifiable movie star."

I laughed. "I don't know about that," I said.

"Sure you are! I saw you on TV, just last night! With my own two eyes!" He glanced down at my leg. "Are you all right?"

"I'm fine." I introduced him to Scott.

"Scott!" Mr. Hornsby said. "I've seen you on TV, too! You're the thriller writer!"

Scott smiled.

"I still haven't had a chance to pick up one of your books," Mr. Hornsby said, scratching his head. "So busy around here."

"What am I, chopped liver?" Cheryl said, under her breath.

"Mr. Hornsby, this is Cheryl Dennison. She's the executive producer of our TV show."

Mr. Hornsby's smile grew wide and he stuck a calloused hand at her. "Well, well, this is certainly a pleasure. You know, love, if you ever want to film a show on almond farming, I'm your man."

Cheryl smiled tightly. "That's an interesting idea."

Mr. Hornsby ran a hand over his graying hair and said, "I can clean up nicely if I have to. We could do a couple episodes down at—"

Out of the corner of my eye, I saw Cheryl wiggle her fingers at me to get me to move the conversation along.

"Mr. Hornsby," I interrupted. "Any idea where my dad could be?"

He blinked at me, a little startled to be pulled out of his farming reality TV fantasy. "Well, it's a little bit of a mystery," he said. "Gordon was here this morning and your friend Becca, too. I saw them driving the bank out wagon around ten thirty this morning, and then I haven't seen them since. But they should have been back by now."

"They should be at the harvester then," I said, ignoring the giant-size pit in my belly that seemed to grow every minute I didn't hear from my dad.

Mr. Hornsby nodded. "That's what I reckoned, too, but I wanted to wait for you here."

"I appreciate that," I said, patting him on the shoulder. "We can take it from here. I'll have my dad call you when he's home, so you know everything's all right."

Mr. Hornsby agreed, then climbed back into his pickup.

I directed Cheryl over to the harvester, and when we arrived Mr. Johnson claimed my father had never gotten there. My stomach felt more unsettled than ever.

"He should have been here by now," I said. "He should have been here at eleven this morning."

Mr. Johnson shrugged. "No, I haven't spoken to him today. We'd talked last night and he told me he'd be in and I was beginning to wonder, but anything's possible. He could have stopped over to the Mucky Duck for lunch and got delayed."

"Dad would never stop for lunch with a full bank out wagon," I insisted.

Mr. Johnson adjusted his bifocals. "I know that," he said, shrugging. "I just don't know what else to think."

It didn't feel right. None of it. It wasn't like my father

to flit off. With a full bank out wagon, he and Becca would have come directly here. Unless, they'd had engine troubles or a tire blew or something unusual had happened. We hadn't seen any accidents on the road over to the harvester.

"Maybe they've been towed to a garage?" I said.

Mr. Johnson nodded. "Let me call over to Gary's, see if he's heard anything." Mr. Johnson walked over to the service desk and picked up the phone.

"Gary Dubuque owns the local garage," I said to Scott and Cheryl.

Scott squeezed my hand. "Don't worry, everything's going to be okay."

Cheryl began to bite her manicured nails, and her bun had completely come undone. Truth be told, she looked like a nervous wreck.

With my free hand, I smacked her fingers away from her mouth, then held on to her hand. "We're going to find him. Everything's going to be fine."

Cheryl clutched my hand. "The psychic, the psychic, he knew!" she cried, her voice getting shrill. "Gordon's in danger."

Mr. Johnson looked up from his phone call and shot Cheryl a confused look.

"Never mind her," I said. "Any luck?"

Mr. Johnson walked back over to us. "No. Gary hasn't gotten any roadside service calls at all today."

I sighed, a feeling of gloom descending on me. If anything happened to my dad and Becca, I'd be lost.

Fifteen

....

INT. CHERYL'S OFFICE DAY

The office is empty. Kyle marches in followed by Ashley.

KYLE
Thank you for putting up with me, darling. I think I'd lose my head if it wasn't attached to me. *(He riffles through a duffel bag near Cheryl's desk.)*

ASHLEY
(smiles) That's okay. I wish you were my stylist all the time. The girl with the tattoos—

KYLE
Lorelei?

ASHLEY
Yeah, that's her. She's okay, but she doesn't have nearly the talent you do.

KYLE
(laughs) That's so kind of you to say. Now, where is it? (He riffles through the duffel bag again, then checks the files on Cheryl's desk.)

ASHLEY
No, seriously. Can you be my permanent stylist? Assign Lorelei to Georgia. She doesn't appreciate you.

KYLE
Oh, she does. She just has a funny way of showing it. Let me give Cheryl a jingle, see where she put my magical curling iron. (He pulls out his cell phone.) Oh, poop! No service. (He pats Ashley on the arm.) I'll be right back. Don't touch a thing. Cheryl can smell when things get reshuffled!
(Kyle leaves the office. Ashley is alone. She riffles through the duffel bag herself, pulls

out a bag of cosmetics and examines several
tubes of lipstick, mascara, and liner. When
she gets bored with the makeup, she looks
down at the desk and sees a folder. Across
the top of the file, in red block print are
the words CONFIDENTIAL: THE TRUTH ABOUT THE
MURDER OF JANE REINER.)

ASHLEY
(gasps) OMG. What do we have here? (She
barely hesitates and rushes to open and read
the folder. As she scans the first page, she
lets out a little yelp and stomps her foot
angrily, then storms out of the office.)

Scott, Cheryl, and I carefully combed the roads back
to my father's farmhouse. Fortunately for us, I knew
where Dad kept his hide-a-key. I went around the back
porch and felt under the third stair.

Cheryl was beside me and she marveled at the grand
house. It was painted white with blue trim and in pristine
condition. Dad was as meticulous with the house as he
was with his farming. Surrounding the porch were large
orange poppies and fragrant blooming jasmine.

Cheryl looked out over our orchids. "You grew up
here, Georgia," she breathed.

"Yup," I said. "Beautiful, right?"

"Breathtaking," she said.

"A little different than L.A.," I agreed. I popped the key out of its hiding place and climbed the porch. "Where's Scott?" I asked.

Cheryl shaded her eyes from the sun as she watched me up on the porch, her feet still planted on the soil. "He's in front. You two okay?"

I shrugged. "Why do you ask?"

"You seem angry with him," she said.

Angry? I was trying to be patient, give him his space but was it coming off as anger? I jammed the key into the lock, almost breaking it, realizing too late that I probably did have quite a bit of anger regarding the whole issue.

But who wouldn't be angry?

I'd cared for him throughout his recovery and loved him more ferociously because of it, knowing how fragile life was and how lucky I was to have such a wonderful man by my side. Through it all, Scott had been strong and funny and brave . . . and now . . . he wasn't sure how he felt about me?

Sure, I was angry!

And to make matters worse, my best friend and my dad were missing! It was a wonder I could see straight. I turned the key in the lock as I wiped tears from my eyes, just in time for Scott to round the corner of the house.

"Oh, good, you found the key," he said, simply.

Cheryl and Scott joined me through the back door into the kitchen.

"Wow," Cheryl breathed. "It's lovely."

Dad had remodeled the kitchen himself recently. There

were granite countertops and handmade cabinets that he and Mr. Hornsby had spent all winter crafting in the garage.

"I'll try them again on the phone," Scott said, alternately dialing my dad then Becca.

I filled up the kettle that perpetually sat on the stove and heated some water.

"I think we should call the police now," Scott said. "They could be injured on the side of the road and we wouldn't even know." His expression was grave and I knew he was thinking about his accident in Spain.

Cheryl paled. "Let's hope not! But I agree, call the police."

I picked up the house phone and dialed Sheriff Bentley. He said he'd be over right away to take our statements. Technically, even though a person had to be missing twenty-four hours, we lived in a small town and Sheriff Bentley knew my father well. He put out an APB right away.

"Maybe we should call Bert again," Cheryl suggested. "Maybe he's had another vision about where Gordon might be."

As ludicrous as it sounded to me, I was willing to try anything and agreed. We called Kyle back at the castle and asked him to get Bert on the line.

"Bert," Cheryl said. "It's very important. We've come back to Gordon's house and he's nowhere to be found. Did you have any more visions of him?"

I heard Cheryl mumble something to him and then turn to me, covering the phone.

"He needs something of Gordon's to see if he can locate him."

"Oh, for crying out loud!" I said. "What is he, a blood-sniffing hound dog?"

Scott patted my shoulder. "Don't lose your patience, Georgia. Everything is going to be fine."

"We should have brought him with us." I said.

Cheryl got a faraway look in her eye.

"Well, do you have anything he gave you?" I asked. "Earrings or a blouse?"

She shrugged. "There may be something in my bag that's in my office."

"Well, send him there. Try that," I said.

Cheryl instructed Bert to go to her trailer office to where her suitcase and gear were. "I think I might have a T-shirt of Gordon's," she said, giving me a strange look, almost as if she didn't want me to know that my father had left clothes with her.

I shrugged my indifference. At this point all that mattered was finding my father and Becca safe.

Bert promised to call us back if he could get a sense of anything.

INT. CHERYL'S OFFICE DAY

The office is empty. Kyle rushes in followed by Bert.

KYLE
I hope they find Gordon and Becca. This is terrible. *(He riffles through the duffel bag*

*near Cheryl's desk and pulls out a man's
shirt.)* Here, will this do?

BERT
(nods) I can try it.

KYLE
Oh, okay. I'll go outside. Give you some
privacy.
*(Kyle leaves the office. Bert is alone. He
sits at the desk and sees the file with the
red block print,* CONFIDENTIAL: THE TRUTH
ABOUT THE MURDER OF JANE REINER. *He waves a
hand over the file and laughs. Then he holds
Gordon's shirt close to his heart. He takes
several deep breaths and closes his eyes.)*

After fifteen minutes of waiting, looking at each other quietly, and drinking tea, we all jumped at the sound of gravel crunching in the front yard. I was the first to reach the front window and see the car.

"Is it them?" Cheryl screeched.

"No, the sheriff," I replied.

Cheryl's shoulders hunched forward, disappointment making her look like a sagging party balloon with a slow leak.

Scott reached out to her. "We're going to find them

tonight! I promise, Cheryl. I'll take the Jeep myself and drive up and down every country road."

I opened the door for the sheriff, just as Cheryl's phone rang. She scrambled to grab it and saw Kyle's phone number on the display. "It must be Bert," she said.

The sheriff took off his hat as he greeted me. I updated him with all the information we had from Mr. Hornsby and Mr. Johnson. I left out the part about the psychic because I figured the sheriff would take that about as seriously as I did.

It didn't help matters when Cheryl picked up the phone, and we all heard Bert's voice through the line.

"I did have a vision," Bert said. "They're on the side of a road."

"Where?" Cheryl asked.

"It's not clear to me. There's trees. Many trees," Bert said.

"Well, we're in the country!" Cheryl shrieked. "There's trees everywhere!"

"These are cherry . . . no . . . no . . . that's not right . . . almond . . . yes almond trees," Bert said.

"Oh, for crying out loud!" Cheryl said.

"Let me talk to him," I said, pulling the phone out of her hand. "Where do you think they are, Bert?"

He said, "They're on the side of the road. They're sitting on the side of the road hitchhiking."

As ridiculous as it sounded, I probed further. "Any idea where? Do you see any identifying landmarks?"

"No," he said, sounding disappointed. "I can't get a clear location."

I handed back the phone to Cheryl and shook my head.

The sheriff frowned. "What's all that about?"

"Our friend, who tends toward psychic abilities, thinks that Gordon and Becca may be hitchhiking."

The sheriff surprised me by rubbing at his chin and looking thoughtful. "He say where?"

"No." I shrugged. "Just the side of the road."

Cheryl hung up. "He's on his way to join us," she announced.

"Well," the sheriff said, "we've got a lot of roads to cover and we're short-staffed." He looked over at Scott and me. "Feel like driving the south side of town, Georgia? I'll take the north side."

I agreed. "Cheryl. You wait here in case Dad comes home."

She nodded and we separated. I took her cell phone so we could be in touch, promising to phone the home line if we found them.

INT. PRAYER ROOM DAY

Dr. Arch is seated in a red-striped high-back chair. He looks especially handsome in a crisp white shirt. He rubs his Roman nose and turns his square jaw at just the right angle for the camera. When he's sure he is looking his best, he leans forward, rests his

chin on his hands, and stares directly into the
camera with his electric blue eyes.

DR. ARCH
(*smiles*) Hello, America. I'm here to caution
you! Karen Kenley and myself are doing our
utmost to solve the murder of Jane Reiner,
but there are others here that are
imposters! Things are not what they seem.
You will see something tonight that will
look horrible. (*He lowers his eyes and looks
remorseful.*) But I assure you . . . cameras
can lie.
Karen and I are getting close to solving
this mystery. (*He glances over his shoulder,
then turns back to the camera, his voice an
urgent whisper.*) The others feel the threat
from us. They know Karen is a serious
investigator and that I am not easily
fooled.
America, please vote for us tonight.

Sixteen
....

Night was falling. The only light on the country road was from our Jeep. Scott and I made our way slowly down the dirt road, backtracking to the harvester, looking for Becca and my father. I held a high-powered searchlight the sheriff had loaned me and scanned the sides of the road, searching for any sign of a tire blowout, fender bender, broken glass, or anything that would give us a clue to where they could be.

Unfortunately, the roads were empty with only a few raccoons scavenging around looking for a nighttime treat.

The search was starting to feel a bit futile.

Scott reached out and touched my leg as he drove. "Are you okay?"

I nodded.

"Things seem awkward between us now," he said. "I'm sorry to have put us in a bad position."

I shook my head. "You haven't put us in a bad position, Scott. You were just being honest."

"I know," he said, "but it seems worse now than before. I probably shouldn't have said anything about how I felt."

Surprise coursed through my body. "The only thing worse than what you said, Scott, would have been to keep it to yourself," I said. "Whatever you're feeling, you have to let me know."

He nodded. "Of course, communication is important in a relationship."

"It is," I said. "I know you're not sure where we are, but I'm going to be patient. I'm going to give you your space just like you asked, and I'm going to be here for you."

He squeezed my knee and said nothing, and I was grateful that he was here next to me, searching Cottonwood for my family.

We drove another half hour in silence. Finally, he turned to me and said, "Do you think we should go back to the house?"

"I don't know what else to do," I said, fighting back the tears that threatened. "I could drive all night looking for them."

He nodded. "Maybe Cheryl's heard something."

The despair in my chest began to overwhelm me, and my throat constricted. "If she had heard something, she would have called."

"That's true," he said.

Suddenly, my phone rang and Cheryl's name came across the display. I hurried to answer it. "Wait a minute! That's her. Fingers crossed."

"Georgia!" Cheryl shouted into the phone. "Get back here."

"What's going on? Are they there?" I asked.

"No, not Gordon or Becca, but Bert's joined me at the farmhouse. He wants to ride along with you and Scott. He thinks he can help you find them."

When we arrived back at my father's house, Mr. Hornsby's pickup truck was parked in the driveway. Bert and Cheryl were standing in front of the house. Cheryl opened my passenger side door and yanked me out of the Jeep.

Bert took my place in the passenger seat, while Cheryl opened the back door, pushed me in, and followed suit.

"Shouldn't you stay here?" I asked. "What if they return?"

"Your father's friend is here. He came over with some dinner for us and to see if we had any news. He'll call me if anything develops," she said. "Anyway, I was going stir-crazy waiting. I'd rather be with you guys when you find them," she said.

The last bit was starting to sound a little like wishful thinking and I admonished myself for being negative. We would find them.

We have to find them!

As Scott pulled out of the driveway, I glimpsed Mr. Hornsby's hopeful face in the window; he was waving at us and nodding. Seeing him fortified my spirit. He believed we could bring them home and I had to believe it, too.

Bert, holding one of my father's flannel shirts, sat with his eyes closed. It felt a little absurd, but I decided to place my faith in him.

Scott asked, "How are you going to tell us where to go if your eyes are closed?"

"Shh," Bert said. "I'm focusing."

"Right," Scott said.

Bert moaned slightly then placed the shirt right up to his nose almost as if he really was a bloodhound on a trail.

Scott turned to look at Cheryl and me in the backseat and said, "I feel like I'm trapped in a Scooby-Doo episode."

"It's a little hard to swallow," I agreed.

Cheryl poked me in the ribs. "Have some faith, Georgia."

"I'm trying," I replied.

Bert moaned louder, then said, "Oh! Turn right up ahead."

Scott slowed down and made a right turn.

"Carry on this way," Bert instructed.

"There's nothing here but orchards," I said.

"Shh," he said.

Oh, goodness.

This was going to be one heck of a ride. He'd take us in circles all night if we let him. I could feel it.

We proceeded down the dirt trail. It was dark with

only the headlights to illuminate the way. The front tire dug into a divot, the Jeep rocking us all.

"The searchlight is in the front seat, Bert," I said. "We can shine—"

Bert's eyes popped open and he whirled around to look at me. "What's Becca's favorite song?"

I glanced at Cheryl, trying to hold on to any patience I had left. This wasn't exactly the time to be trying to get to know my best friend better. "What's it matter?" I asked him.

"Just tell me. Sing it," he said.

Sing it?

Oh, for crying out loud.

Cheryl jabbed me again in the ribs, this time with intent to injure. "Don't be so difficult, Georgia. Sing her favorite song."

I shrugged. "I don't know what her favorite song is. She likes all types of music."

"Dolly Parton. She likes Dolly Parton," Scott said, from the front seat.

That much was true. Becca was a huge country music fan, but I was a little stunned that Scott had been the one to come up with the answer.

"'Coat of Many Colors,'" he continued. "That's her favorite song."

"How do you know?" I asked him.

He shrugged. "She told me once."

"She told you?" I asked, shocked. How could Scott know my best friend better than I did?

"We were up late talking, and a Dolly Parton special

came on. Dolly said her favorite song was 'Coat of Many Colors,' and then Becca told me it was her favorite, too."

"Aww," Bert said. And even though I couldn't see his expression in the dark, I figured he was a little moon-eyed for Becca right now.

"All right, people, let's focus," I said. "This nonsense isn't going to help us find them." I strained to see out the window.

Bert said, "I love Dolly Parton. I love Becca."

I punched him in the arm. "Would you stop? We need to get back to the task of finding them."

"I'm sorry," he said. "I was overwhelmed by emotion."

"Why don't we turn left?" I said to Scott. "I think we're getting close to the south side of town and that's the part the sheriff is searching. I don't want to waste our—"

"Don't turn yet," Bert said.

Scott slowed the Jeep. "Folks, we have to agree. Georgia, what if I take you back to the house. Maybe you can borrow Mr. Hornsby's truck—"

"Good idea! Or what about . . . Bert, did you drive down? What car did you bring? I can take—"

Bert held up his hands "Stop. Please! Stop chattering and sing."

"What?" I asked. "Sing what?"

"'Coat of Many Colors,'" he replied.

"What's that going to do?" I asked, not even attempting to keep the disdain out of my voice.

"It'll help. I promise," he said. "We'll find them soon. I think we're close."

Oh, brother. This psychic business was just too much.

Cheryl didn't wait for a second invitation. She began to belt out "Coat of Many Colors." Scott snickered, and I did all I could to keep my temper in check.

"Turn left up ahead," Bert said.

The irony struck me, that turning left was just the thing I'd said to do, but I bit my tongue.

Scott turned and soon we were on another road. This road was a little wider and more of a major thoroughfare than the one we'd just been on. Within a few minutes, two figures came into view, walking down the trail.

Oh, my god.

My heart nearly leapt out of my chest.

As we slowly rolled down the road, the two figures stopped and looked into the headlights and waved madly.

It was my father and Becca!

Scott honked and flashed the headlights. He stopped the car, and we all tumbled out, rushing toward them.

"Dad! Dad! Becca!" I yelled, racing to get to them.

Cheryl reached my father first and hugged him fiercely. I hugged them both and soon the six of us were all huddled in a group embrace.

"What happened?" I asked. "What are you doing down this road?"

Becca grabbed my arms. "Oh, my God, Georgia. It was terrible," she said. "We were carjacked!"

"What?" Scott asked.

"My almond harvest was hijacked," Dad said.

"How can that be?" Cheryl asked.

"Two bearded men with guns," Becca said. "They took Gordon's full bank out wagon. They forced us out of the truck at gunpoint. They took our phones, everything," Becca said. "It was horrible. Thank God, I was with Gordon or I would have peed my pants!"

Bert laughed and hugged her. All of a sudden, Becca was overcome with embarrassment and flushed bright red.

"I'm so glad you're safe," Cheryl said. "We've been worried sick."

Something niggled at me.

How had Bert known where to find Becca and my father? How had he even known they'd been in danger? Could he really be psychic?

I closed the distance between us and grabbed Bert's arm. "Thank you for helping us."

He patted my hand, and smiled. "I'm glad I was able to help." He shrugged. "Sometimes I am, and sometimes I'm not. That makes people wonder about me, but it's not like I'm a computer, you know? I don't really know how or why inspiration hits me, but when it does watch out."

He speech seemed to move Becca, because she clutched at him and said, "They blindfolded us and tied us up."

"Give themselves a little time to get away with my harvest, I suspect," Dad grumbled.

"Oh, Dad," I said, collapsing into his arms. "All your hard work. The season. Your whole season!"

He squeezed me tight. "We were heading toward Old Man Stone's house. Going to ask him to call the sheriff from there."

"Feels like we've been walking for hours," Becca said.

"Stone's house is still at least seven miles," I said.

"I know," Becca said. "I have blisters on my blisters."

"What are you all doing here?" Dad asked. "How did you know we were in trouble?"

I shifted around awkwardly. "Well, that's a story in and of itself. Let's get home and let the sheriff know we found you."

Back at my father's house, Mr. Hornsby was delighted to heat the supper his wife had prepared for us: a hearty bowl of homemade split-pea soup and a fresh loaf of bread.

When we reported the carjacking to the sheriff, he surprised us by saying my father was the third almond farmer in the area to make such a report.

"The draught really wreaked havoc in the area," the sheriff said.

"Almond prices are sky-high right now," Dad agreed.

"A shortage does that," Scott said.

"You got insurance, Gordon?" the sheriff asked.

Dad snorted. "Sure, but they only guarantee last year's price."

Cheryl groaned. "Gordon, I'm so sorry."

Dad and Becca gave the sheriff as many details on the men as they could, and Sheriff Bentley promised to do his best to catch the ring of thieves.

As soon as he left, Cheryl said, "Well, I don't know if

anyone is in the mood, but we do have an episode airing . . ."

Becca screeched and dove for the remote control. "Of course, we're in the mood!"

"Should I pop popcorn?" Scott asked.

"I got it," Mr. Hornsby called from the kitchen.

Becca flipped on the TV to a commercial break.

"I have it on DVR," Dad said.

Becca quickly navigated to the beginning of the episode. The opening was shots from the previous episode, including my feet dangling through the third floor. My leg stung just watching the replay of it.

Scott pulled me onto his lap and nuzzled his chin into my shoulder. "I hate seeing that! How are you feeling now?"

"I'm fine," I said, enjoying the closeness of him. "I feel better just knowing that Dad and Becca are all right."

The episode unfolded quickly, with the elimination of Father Gabriel and Martha, followed by the *Jeopardy*-style game.

When I saw Father Gabriel, I was reminded all over again that I hadn't had a chance to speak with him after his elimination. A heaviness filled me, as if the lost opportunity was costing me a price yet undetermined.

The next scene was of me in Cheryl's office. I sat to attention as the image of me looking at the file with the red block print flashed across the screen, *CONFIDENTIAL: THE TRUTH ABOUT THE MURDER OF JANE REINER.*

Scott gasped. "Hell!" He shot an angry look at Cheryl

and Becca. "Is this some kind of sick joke? You all already know who murdered Jane!"

Cheryl waved a hand at him. "It's not what you think."

"Not what I think?" Scott demanded.

"It's a setup," Bert said.

We turned back to the screen; Harris's velvety voice narrated the scene. "America! Each team was given an opportunity to cheat. This is a test of their character. Remember, you will ultimately decide which team is the most fit to solve this cold case in the castle."

On the screen, the image of me not opening the file changed to Bert doing the same, then next to Ashley, who opened the file, and ending with Dr. Arch opening the file to reveal the word *CHEATER!*

I'd figured it had been a setup, but I had a slight advantage in that I knew the producer of the show. But how had Bert known?

The episode ended with Dr. Arch's appeal to the audience, claiming things were not as they seemed. In other words, maintaining he wasn't a cheater.

"Ha!" Becca said. "You think people are really going to buy that?"

Cheryl shrugged. "He's got a large following. I'm anxious to get back and find out how the votes are going."

"We can all go in the morning," Dad said, taking her hand.

Cheryl smiled and for the first time she looked relaxed.

Seventeen
....

The following morning, Becca, my dad, Bert, Scott, Cheryl, and I drove out to the Golden Castle. When we arrived, we were surprised to find the head of the historical society, Gertrude, with an older gentleman in tow. The man wore spectacles and had gray hair and a stern expression on his face.

They stood on the front porch, blocking our entrance. The man handed Cheryl a letter as soon as Gertrude said, "That's her, that's the one."

He pushed the spectacles farther up the bridge of his nose, and said, "Uh, miss, I'm Daniel Lowenstein. I'm going to have to ask you and your crew to suspend productions until we can get the matter of the third floor sorted out."

"What's going on?" my father asked.

Cheryl huffed. "You can't be serious. We're in the middle of a production here. We're not going to hold up our film schedule because of the third floor. We don't even need access to that floor."

"I understand, ma'am," Daniel said. "It's just that Ms. Gertrude is very upset with all the destruction going on in the castle. I'm afraid we're going to have to . . ." He glanced over at Gertrude as if to get strength from her. When she glared back at him, he continued. "We had an emergency board meeting, and we're going to have to rescind the access we've allowed you."

"This is absurd!" Cheryl said.

Guilt wrapped its ugly tentacles through my sternum and squeezed. This was because of me. My going up to the third floor had caused the damage. Scott put a hand on my shoulder, seeming to realize the distress I was feeling.

"It's not your fault," he whispered into my ear.

I thought again about my trip up to the third floor. Kyle had sent me. Why? Someone had sent him a text, but to what avail? Was someone trying to get me out of the way?

Dr. Arch had been upstairs and denied it. He'd been outside by the pool the evening the groundskeeper had been killed. His plea from the previous evening's show reverberated in my mind. He'd said things were not as they seemed.

Could he be the one who wanted me out of the way?

My father took the paperwork out of Cheryl's hands. "I'm sure we can get this straightened out while you get your cast ready for production. What do you have, a few more episodes to film?"

Cheryl nodded.

"Certainly we can negotiate something," my father said to Mr. Lowenstein.

"No, we are absolutely firm about this," Gertrude said, her gray bouffant bouncing as she spoke. A few curls escaped and stood straight up on the top of her head, almost looking like horns. "Pack up your things," she screeched. "You all must be out of here by evening tonight." She turned on a heel and stormed away.

Mr. Lowenstein tracked after Gertrude like a lost puppy.

"It's impossible," Cheryl said. "I'm going to ignore her. If RTV Studios calls me, then I'll listen, but for now Gertrude is just background noise."

"Maybe we can work something out," Becca said. "Get some shots inside and film the rest of the episodes on the grounds at large, and we won't disturb the castle."

Cheryl scratched her chin. "Yes, something like that. It's a thought. Let's at least get our filming done now, see how much we can get in the can for the episode that airs tonight. I'll have Mr. Martin, our Hollywood attorney, reach out to Lowenstein, see if he can work some magic." She glanced at her watch, shaking her head in frustration. "We're frightfully behind schedule. I don't even have the status of the votes from last night. Not to mention, our second elimination is already behind schedule."

My father got a sour look on his face. "I'm sorry you're behind schedule because of me."

"Don't be ridiculous," Cheryl said. She pushed open the door to the castle to reveal the cast and crew scrambling about. "Kyle!" Cheryl screamed.

Becca looked around. It appeared that not even the breakfast buffet had been served. "My goodness, it's anarchy here. You really do need me," she said to Cheryl.

"We do need you," Bert said. "We need you!" His cheeks turned rosy when she smiled at him.

"I'll arrange the food service," Becca said to Cheryl.

Cheryl nodded distractedly as if feeding the cast and crew was the last thing on her mind.

My father kissed her cheeks, then put one arm around her shoulders and the other around mine. "Listen, ladies, I know you're going to be very busy here. I'll head over to the Indian resort and get out of the way."

Cheryl pointed a finger at him. "No gambling!"

Dad laughed. "You got enough of a gamble going on here for the both of us. I'm going to lounge at the pool."

Once Dad retreated, Cheryl clapped her hands in an authoritative manner. "Folks! Listen up! Get into hair and makeup immediately! We need to film the elimination right away!"

Within a few minutes we were lined up in front of Harris. He held some cream-colored envelopes that Kyle had handed him. I assumed inside the envelopes were the results from the vote the night before. Strangely, my nerves tensed. Scott and I hadn't had a big piece in last night's episode.

Would we be voted off?

Standing next to me, Scott pressed his lips together and stared straight ahead.

Ashley wiggled and studied her fingernails, while Jessica smiled nervously. Dr. Arch and Karen looked relaxed and confident. Jack, the ghost hunter, tapped his foot repeatedly, but Bert seemed at peace.

On Cheryl's cue, Harris came to life. "Hello, America!" his voice resounded through the room. "Welcome back to *Cold Case in the Castle*! Where we're committed to getting to the bottom of the unsolved murder of Jane Reiner. Last night, your votes poured in again and"—he tapped the envelopes he held—"I'm ready to reveal the results."

Harris peeled open the first envelope and silently read the names. He then made a dramatic show of assessing us, as the cameras rolled past us, capturing our nervous expressions.

"Dr. Arch, Karen Kenley!" Harris called out. The camera zoomed in close on their faces. "Your fans from *Hunting Bones* did not disappoint! Again, they called in droves to support you. They are confident you can solve the cold case! You are safe from elimination."

Karen flashed a cocky smile and Dr. Arch simply nodded his agreement with his fans. Indeed, he thought he was the best person to solve the case, as well.

"Jessica, Ashley!" Harris called out. The girls squirmed.

"America thinks it's wise to keep the grand-niece of the victim on board to solve the crime. Therefore, you are safe from elimination."

Jessica clamped a hand over her mouth and squealed, then let out a rush of air. "I'm so happy. I know my great-aunt died far too young and has waited a long time for justice. I hope we can get her that."

Harris drew a breath and ripped open the next envelope. He looked at us. "Scott and Georgia. Bert and Jack. One team will be leaving the castle immediately."

Bert looked grim, and grabbed my hand. "It was nice to meet you, Georgia. Good luck solving the mystery. I know you will."

Harris cleared his throat. "Uh. Excuse me. I haven't announced who is leaving yet."

"It's Jack and I," Bert said. He thumped Jack on the back. "Sorry about that."

Harris's nose flared and he looked around the room for Cheryl. "Can we retake that? This guy is stealing my thunder."

Cheryl laughed. "Just keep rolling. We don't have time for another take."

Harris's lips turned into a thin line, and I swore I could see fumes coming out of his ears. "Scott, Georgia," Harris boomed. "You are safe from elimination." Then he turned to sneer at Bert. "Bert, Jack. The viewers have spoken, and they don't think you're capable of solving this mystery. Please say your good-byes immediately!"

Jack shook Scott's hand. "Good luck. I know you and

Georgia can do this." He handed him the voltmeter. "You'll need this."

"Hey!" Karen called out. "Is that fair?"

Jack shrugged. "Is it fair that Dr. Arch and Ashley tried to read a confidential file and are still on the show?"

Ashley blushed, but Dr. Arch remained aloof.

"What file?" Jessica asked.

Jack waved a hand, signaling his farewell. "Ask them," he said, as he turned on a heel and left the room.

Bert put an arm around my shoulders and pressed me into his large frame. "You can do this. Just believe." He said good-bye to the others, and followed Jack out of the room.

A wave of disappointment flooded me. I'd really begun to like Jack and Bert. After all, finding my dad and Becca may not have been possible without Bert, and now they were gone.

Scott laced his fingers through mine. "Let's solve this thing, G."

Harris clapped his hands together to get our attention. "Folks, yesterday we played a *Jeopardy*-style game and you were given access to parts of the castle previously unexplored. Now you will have the opportunity to investigate those areas."

Scott and I, with our cameraman, Adam, in tow, set off to examine the kitchen. We reached the kitchen using a rickety spiral staircase from the dining room. I gripped the rail as we descended.

"The kitchen is below the dining room? What sense does that make?" I asked.

Scott shrugged. "I think that's pretty typical of the era this was built in. They didn't have grocery stores and stuff, you know. They grew everything in the fields and then brought it in on ground level."

"Right," I agreed. "But then how did they serve the prepared food? By running up and down these awful stairs?"

Scott laughed. "It was a reform school. I suppose the boys on KP really felt punished."

Downstairs, the kitchen was poorly lit, with one small dirty window that just barely cleared ground level. I shivered. It was depressing down here and I couldn't imagine being one of the small boys on duty.

The tile floors were badly chipped and worn. The antique oven was almost in pristine condition, but burn marks scarred the cubbies and pantry where the supplies had been stored. Now, everything was barren and desolate.

"Can you imagine cooking in some place like this?" I asked.

"You probably can't imagine cooking anywhere," Scott teased.

I jabbed his chest. "Shut up! I'm a pretty good cook."

He rubbed the sore spot on his pecs. "You are? Have you made me anything? All I remember is Chinese takeout."

Regret rolled through me.

What kind of girlfriend was I? Hadn't I ever cooked for him?

"I make a great eggplant lasagna," I said.

Scott smiled. "Maybe you'll cook it for me sometime." He rubbed at his stomach. "Man, all this food talk is just making me hungry."

I opened and closed the door to the wood-burning oven. "It must have been a lot of work to keep this thing lit."

"Yeah," Scott agreed. "It probably took a whole team of people. But I guess the rehabilitation program really worked. When kids left here they had skills. They could do something with their lives."

I nodded. "It is important to have skills," I said, wondering about my own.

Where would I get work after this show was over?

After all, reality TV show cast member isn't really something you can put on a regular resume, is it?

Scott approached a small cubbyhole, and the voltmeter secured on his belt loop let out a sharp beep.

"Whoa! What's that?" I asked.

"This is where her body was recovered," Scott said, examining the cubbyhole.

I recognized the cubbyhole from some of the initial information Cheryl had given the cast. I leaned in close to Scott and studied the small space. The wood was stained and rotted through. There was a blanket and pillow stuffed inside as if someone at some point had taken a nap in there.

The voltmeter squawked louder, and the hair on the back of my neck stood on end.

"Spooky," I whispered.

Scott shifted so I could lean in closer and then put his hand under my chin. He tilted my face toward him. "Are you scared, G?"

There was a mischievous twinkle in his eyes that I welcomed, and as I pressed my forehead to his, the voltmeter nearly exploded with sound.

He jumped away from me and looked at the device. There were several blue and yellow lights flashing. "What does it even mean?" he asked.

I laughed. "I don't know. You suppose there's some ghostly energy around us?"

He shrugged, and turned the device off. "Hey. What about that DNA kit you ended up with in the last challenge? Do you want to swab some stuff?"

Would it do any good?

The truth was, I'd only taken a DNA sample in the police academy. Reading DNA hadn't been a part of my job as a communications officer, but I figured it might make for good TV. So I pulled the kit out and swabbed around the cubbyhole.

Adam, the cameraman, got in close as I put the solution onto the wood and then dabbed it away with my kit. "Maybe I can ask Karen if she can take a look at this for us," I said.

Although, after all these years and so many cooks in the kitchen, so to speak, I didn't know what kind of DNA evidence would even be available on the slides. I packaged everything up and put it in my kit.

"Oh, yeah," Scott said sarcastically. "Karen seems really eager to help us." He wandered around the corner and poked at a small box in the wall of the pantry. "Look at this."

"What is it?" I asked.

"A dumbwaiter," Scott said, yanking on one of the pulleys.

"Wow. So that's how they got the meals upstairs, huh?" Scott nodded. "Pretty cool."

"Is it big enough to hold a body?" I asked.

Scott shuddered. "Geez, Georgia! And you're always accusing me of being grim."

I pushed at him playfully. "Oh, shut it!"

He scooped me into his arms and teased, "Well, let's see if it's big enough to hold a body. I'm sure I can stuff you in."

I climbed into the dumbwaiter. "I fit."

Scott looked amazed. "You are tiny!"

I laughed. "Just because I have a big mouth doesn't mean I have a big . . ." I bit my lip and looked over at Adam, who was smiling. "Never mind." I pressed my palms against the cold wood, and shivers ran down my arms as I imagined poor Jane in this coffin-like box.

I fumbled with the pulley system. "Can you hoist me up?"

"What?" Scott demanded. "To the third level, so you can fall through that big crater that used to be a floor?"

I cringed. "Right, bad idea!" I tumbled out of the dumbwaiter and looked over at Adam.

He nodded at me, indicating he had the footage he needed. I was happy. Hopefully, people climbing into ancient dumbwaiters would make good TV.

We made our way out of the kitchen, climbing the spiral staircase back to the dining room. The dining room was empty, but in the corridor we ran into Jessica and Ashley.

"Look at what we found," Jessica said excitedly. She motioned toward a box of envelopes.

"What is it?" Scott asked.

"Letters. Old letters. We have to search through them! Come on! We need a little help sorting everything out," Ashley said.

Scott pulled out a chair for me to sit, then took the chair next to me. We agreed to read and sort through the pile, sharing anything relevant.

In the silence, I remembered my dream about Jane. She'd written a letter to her mother . . . about something she'd seen . . . could it be that perhaps her mother had written back?

Eighteen

....

We sorted through the letters for quite a while. While the others quietly read, I was stuck pondering the dumbwaiter. Something about it nagged at me. I wanted to explore it a bit more, but knew Scott wouldn't go for it.

How far did the dumbwaiter go?

Certainly to the dining room, but did it end there or go further up? Had I seen a dumbwaiter up on the third floor? I racked my brain to try to recall the third floor, but I came up empty.

I leaned into Scott. "I think I might try to hunt for Dr. Arch and Karen."

He nodded, barely looking up from the letter he was reading.

Jessica and Ashley seemed equally absorbed in their reading. As I stood, Adam picked his camera up and stood, leaving the cameraman assigned to Jessica and Ashley to keep filming.

Ditching Adam was going to be a problem.

I knew I absolutely wasn't supposed to go upstairs, but I slunk down the corridor to the staircase anyway. There I hesitated, deciding to go down or up. Dr. Arch and Karen were in the basement, so I should have headed down the stairs. Instead, I glanced at Adam.

He groaned.

"I'm going up," I whispered.

"Oh, for Pete's sake, Georgia. You want to get me fired?" Adam whined.

"Tell her I gave you the slip."

"Telling Cheryl that will get me fired. Let's just go back to the library," he said.

Scott poked his head out of the library. "Hey, Georgia. We found something interesting. There's a mention of another death in one of the letters. Three weeks prior to Jane's murder. Come take a look." He retreated back to the library and Adam happily followed him.

Seizing my moment of solitude, I crept up to the second floor and moved close to where I figured would be right on top of the kitchen and dining room. Sure enough, the dumbwaiter was there. Could I make it to the third floor and examine where the dumbwaiter led? Could it have led to the victim's bedroom?

What would that tell me?

The third floor beckoned me like a siren to a sailor. There was something on the third floor I needed to see, even if I didn't know what it was. Even Dr. Arch and Father Gabriel had been intrigued by the third floor, although they wouldn't admit it.

I crept cautiously up the stairs, promising myself I would stop if it didn't seem safe. I tiptoed up the rotted staircase and peeked out into the hallway. I was saddened to see the cavernous hole in the floor that I had caused. It seemed beyond repair, and that thought left a similar-feeling hole in my heart.

Then something down the hallway caught my eye. Something shimmery.

What was it?

It glittered like little gems in the light that poured in from the window.

And then it hit me; the window was broken.

Glass!

It hadn't been here before, or else I hadn't noticed it. I carefully made my way toward it. A breeze fluttered through the gaping broken window. Had the bird migration from the first day caused this? I crept toward it to examine it further. I peered out the window and my breath caught.

Through the window, down three stories, was a crumpled body.

Oh, dear God, no!

I whipped around to run toward the stairwell when Dr. Arch stepped out of one of the bedrooms, startling me.

Clamping a hand over my madly beating heart, I demanded, "What are you doing up here?" My voice was high-pitched, caught between anger and fear.

Wasn't he supposed to be in the basement with Karen?

"I could ask you the same thing," he said. The look on his face was difficult to read, but his posture was challenging me.

How long had he been up here? Could he have pushed the victim out the window?

"There's been an accident," I said, pointing toward the window. "Look!"

He frowned, then crossed over to examine the window. His heavy shoes crunched on the glass and then I noticed he was holding his hand awkwardly, protectively in toward his body.

Was he injured?

Dr. Arch caught me noticing his arm and dropped it by his side, then he saw the body below. His face registered shock.

"Oh, my goodness! Who is that?" he asked

"I don't know. Someone dressed in black."

The terrible thought struck me that the victim could be Father Gabriel, but how was that possible? Hadn't he already left the castle yesterday?

Together, Dr. Arch and I rushed downstairs. I was grateful that I didn't cause any further damage to the third floor, but I knew Gertrude would be upset about the broken window. Forget about the dead body, that woman was cold and she likely wouldn't give a flying hoot about the poor victim.

We took the stairs two by two and when I hit the bottom

step, the wooden board cracked under my weight. Thankfully the banister held me.

Dr. Arch pushed past me. "You are accident prone, aren't you?"

"What about you?" I pressed. "How did you hurt your arm?"

"My arm is fine," he lied.

I ignored him and raced on to get to the body. As we rushed past the library, Scott popped out in the hallway and called, "What's going on?"

Adam was right behind him, with his camera focused on me.

"Call 911," I screamed, as I ran out toward the front door.

Adam groaned, as he fumbled for his phone. Scott followed Dr. Arch and me outside to the front porch and then around the side of the castle to where the body lay crumpled on the grass.

I was first to the body. The grass was wet around his head. I assumed it was perhaps blood that had sopped into the earth. Shards of glass covered the back of his cassock. "Don't touch anything. Don't touch anything," I yelled as Scott and Dr. Arch joined me.

Dr. Arch ignored me and flipped the body over. It was definitely Father Gabriel. There was a large angry gash across Father Gabriel's forehead, probably caused by the impact from the fall that had killed him.

"I have to try," Dr. Arch said, pressing his fingers into Father Gabriel's limp wrist. "Nothing," he said sadly.

I refrained from scolding him. After all, I supposed he had a Hippocratic oath he had to abide by. At least it wasn't me messing up a potential crime scene this time.

What had Father Gabriel been doing here?

Sorrow filled me as I looked down at the dead priest. Tears stung at my eyes, and Scott pulled me into an embrace.

"I'm so sorry," he said, "I'm so sorry, Georgia."

I held on to Scott as I surveyed the area. Father Gabriel was sprawled on top of a grassy knoll that rolled all the way from the castle to the perimeter of the rosebushes. Near the bushes was an old rusty wheelbarrow that seemed pushed out of the way.

There was nothing all that remarkable in sight.

Voices sounded behind us as Cheryl, my father, and Becca raced toward us.

"What's going on?" Cheryl screeched. When she saw Father Gabriel, a string of expletives rushed out of her mouth and then she glared at me as if I was the source of all the bad luck.

Maybe I was.

Before long Officer Holtz arrived to investigate. I recounted for him my steps, including the fact that I'd been on the third floor.

He tapped on his notebook, only mildly interested, but Cheryl gasped. "What? Georgia! You know the third floor is off limits!"

"Well . . ." I stammered. "I saw broken glass."

She frowned at me. "From where?"

"From down the hall," I admitted.

Cheryl gave me the "you're hopeless" look, but said nothing.

Officer Holtz looked from Cheryl and then back at me. He squinted. "All right, so you were up there and you saw the broken glass and then what?"

I pointed at Dr. Arch. "Then I saw him."

Cheryl whipped around and glared at Dr. Arch. "You, too! What were you doing on the third floor?"

Officer Holtz turned red-faced. "I ask the questions around here!"

Cheryl looked chagrined and retreated to my father's side.

"How about you, doc? How long were you up on the third floor? Did you see anything?"

Dr. Arch grimaced. "I didn't see anything helpful. What I saw was Georgia skulking up the stairs alone. No camera—"

"What!" Cheryl demanded, "Where is Adam?"

Regret filled my belly. Why had I gone up to the third floor in the first place?

"I thought she was cheating," Dr. Arch continued. "After all, we weren't supposed to go up to the third floor. So I followed her to see if she had any inside information on the Jane Reiner mystery."

"No. That's wrong," I said. "You were up on the third floor before I was. You came out of one of the rooms."

He shook his head, looking offended. "No, I didn't."

"And your hand." I pointed accusingly at him. "You're

hurt. What? Was it the struggle with Father Gabriel as you pushed him out the window?"

Officer Holtz held up a hand. "That's enough." He got close to my face, his sour coffee breath burning my nostrils. "I've already told you. SFPD is not handling this investigation. I am," he growled.

Nineteen

....

Becca had ordered Mexican food for the buffet, and even as news about Father Gabriel spread, shocking the cast, it didn't seem to slow down anyone's appetite.

As we dipped tortilla chips into guacamole, the crime scene techs cordoned off the upstairs. I craned my neck to watch men in white suits swab the banister.

Suddenly, Gertrude raced into the hallway. "What's going on?" she screeched at one of the techs.

I didn't hear his mumbled reply, but in response Gertrude said, "Absolutely not! No one is allowed on the third floor. It's unsafe! I demand a search warrant and a liability waiver before anyone can poke around up there!"

Officer Holtz was systematically questioning members of the cast and crew in the library. He must have heard

Gertrude's ruckus because he peeked into the hallway and called her over.

I resisted the urge to follow and eavesdrop, but just barely.

Next to me, Jessica ladled some refried beans on top of a flour tortilla. "Poor Father Gabriel. I can't imagine him falling through the window. Something is going on here. Do you think a ghost pushed him?"

"I don't think that's possible, dear," Karen Kenley said, shuffling past her to grab the salsa and cheddar cheese. "But you can certainly share that theory with the investigating officer when it's your turn. I'm sure he'll be fascinated with it."

"Why wouldn't that be possible?" Ashley demanded. "I bet Father Gabriel snuck up to the third floor to try to clear it of spirits and they had other ideas."

I listened to the ladies argue as they piled food on their plates. First the carne asada, then some *carnitas*, black beans, sour cream, guacamole, all of it stacking into delectable burritos. My stomach rumbled, but I was more interested in food as fuel than as a gossip hub.

Next to me, Scott was quiet and subdued as he sampled the tilapia.

"Scott, before we found Father Gabriel, you said something about a mention of another death in one of the letters. Prior to Jane's murder. What was it?"

Scott glanced over toward Karen Kenley and whispered, "Not in front of her." Then he took his plate over to one of the tables to wait for me.

So they'd found something that could help us solve Jane's murder.

Was Jane's murder connected to Father Gabriel's and the groundskeeper's deaths? It had to be. What had Father Gabriel known? Had he seen something here in the castle? On the third floor? What had he been looking for?

As I pondered these questions, Becca came up behind me and asked, "Don't you like the food?"

"It looks awesome," I said, quickly assembling a taco salad. "Have you given your statement to Officer Holtz yet?" I asked.

She nodded. "Yeah, he wanted the crew's break schedule and stuff, which I was happy to give him, but I don't know how much that will help. We're strict on running background checks on everyone . . ." She sighed. "Poor Father Gabriel. Anyway . . ." She glanced over her shoulder and asked, "What do you think of Bert? He's so nice, right?"

I followed her gaze toward the door and saw Bert standing there. "Is he still here? I thought he and Jack left."

"Jack did. But Bert wanted to hang out a little longer." She wiggled her shapely brows at me in a way that suggested she was very excited about the prospect.

I snorted. "I can't believe you're seriously interested in the lumberjack psychic."

"He's super sweet," Becca said.

"Was he in the castle today?" I asked.

Becca frowned. "What do you mean?"

"After he got voted off and left. Did he come back in?"

She shook her head. "No, he ran into town with me to order the food for you guys." She waved a hand over the buffet. "Why?"

"I guess he wasn't wandering around upstairs on the third floor pushing a priest out a window then," I said.

Becca made no attempt to hide the shock that crossed her face. "Georgia!"

I shrugged. "Don't be offended. It's just my SFPD training."

All right, so Bert may have an alibi for today, but I still didn't know Father Gabriel's time of death. It had to have been today, though, I reasoned. His body was in plain sight. Otherwise someone would have seen him earlier.

"I heard from the producers of *Globe Tracker* again," Becca said. "They think you're brilliant. That you fell through the floor on purpose to garner sympathy and support from your fans. You just need to make it through one more elimination and the job's yours."

I glanced over at the table where Scott was waiting for me. "I need some answers on Jane's murder if we have a chance of solving this," I said.

Becca nodded. "Okay. Go do your thing. We'll catch up later." Then she practically skipped over to the doorway where Bert was waiting for her. Together they left the room. Now, only the three teams that remained, Dr. Arch and Karen Kenley, Ashley and Jessica, Scott and I, were in the room. Each couple sat at separate tables as if the competition was getting too serious now.

I joined Scott, who sat solemnly swirling his food.

"Don't you like the tilapia?" I asked.

He looked up startled. "Oh, it's fine. I was just lost in thought."

"About what?" I probed.

He rubbed at his shaved head. "At all the craziness going on around us." He lowered his voice and leaned in close to me. "These deaths . . . they have to be connected. Whoever murdered Jane is trying to stop us from figuring it out. Stop this show from airing . . ."

"You think so?" I asked.

He nodded.

"But how can that be? Her murder was almost fifty years ago."

"Well, that doesn't make it impossible, but if it's not the same murderer, it's someone trying to protect them. A family member or something. Son or daughter."

I mentally started to calculate ages of the contestants. "It could be anyone, though. Like Dr. Arch or something. We don't know anything about him. His father could have attended here as a boy, right?"

"Right," Scott agreed. "And we know Father Gabriel was enrolled here as a youth, but now we can't ask him . . ." His voice trailed off.

"Tell me about what you found earlier," I whispered.

"There was another death," Scott said. "A boy named Merle Greens drowned in the river. He was seventeen. Had been convicted of shoplifting. He'd been at the school for six months. Was getting close to being released. He worked in the kitchen."

"But what could that have to do with Jane's death?" I asked.

"I don't know," Scott admitted. "Some of the letters referred to him. He was friendly with a lot of people it seems."

"Was he friends with Jane?" I asked.

Scott shrugged. "I couldn't tell from any of the letters. Jessica said she knew about Merle because of the town's history. I guess they have a plaque at city hall with the names of all victims the river has claimed. But she said she never heard her mom talk about Merle in any connection to Jane."

I fidgeted next to him, impatient for more concrete information. "Any specifics about the drowning?"

The corners of Scott's mouth turned down. "From what little I read, it seemed like an accident."

After dinner, Cheryl stormed into the dining hall and announced, "All right, folks. We know some strange things are going on around here, but as you know, the show must go on."

There was a little rumbling through the cast, but mostly I think their energy mirrored my own. We were anxious to get the show on the road.

"We're going to proceed with the voting tonight. There will be an elimination in the morning. However, we're still a bit short on footage for the episode tonight. I'm going to have you give your pleas directly to the audience. Live." She gave the cast her most serious "I mean business" look, then landed on me. "I expect professionalism out of each and every one of you."

I put a hand on my heart, ready to profess whatever she needed, but she waved me away. "Oh, save it, Georgia!"

Kyle and his makeup team appeared to touch everyone up. Harris strutted onto the set, making a show of looking at his watch. "The union will hear about this," he huffed.

Cheryl put on her headset and glared at him. "Can it, you oaf, or I'll have Kyle make you look orange."

Harris's eyes popped wide open and his mouth downturned. "You wouldn't dare!"

"Try me," Cheryl fired back. When Harris didn't reply, she motioned the camera, lights, and sound team into action.

Harris took a deep breath and squared his shoulders to the cameras. "Hello, America!" he boomed. "And welcome back to *Cold Case in the Castle*. This evening we're going to ask you to vote for your favorite team. As you know, only three teams remain. Dr. Arch and Karen Kenley; Jessica, the grand-niece of our poor victim, Jane Reiner, and her partner, the ever-fearless paranormal docent Ashley. And then America's favorite couple, from the hit TV show *Love or Money*, Scott and Georgia."

Good Lord! Harris was in full melodramatic mode. The threat from Cheryl to turn him orange must have motivated him to really ham it up.

The cameras panned the cast and I noticed stiff smiles coming from Ashley and Jessica. Even Karen flipped her black hair at the camera and flashed her white teeth. Dr. Arch seemed curiously subdued and I realized he was holding his arm across his body, favoring the hand again.

What was going on with him?

While the camera was on us, a crew member handed Harris a small item I couldn't immediately identify. Harris stuck the item under one arm, then clapped his hands together and held them in a small triangle in front of his chest. "Only three teams remain, America. And we haven't gotten any closer to solving the murder of Jane Reiner! Tonight, we'll ask each team to plead their case with you. Why they should remain on the show and be able to investigate further. At stake is this—" He whipped out the item and waved it at the camera.

I squinted.

What was it?

It looked like a microchip for a computer.

"*This* will enable the winners to have one hour online to research and investigate any possible leads for Jane's murder," Harris said. "Including access to old police records." He held the drive card up in front of us all.

Scott leaned into me. "Do you know how to use that?" he asked.

"Yup," I said. "You stick it in the drive and read. Hopefully, there's something worthwhile on it."

INT. LIBRARY NIGHT

Jessica and Ashley are seated in two high-back chairs. Jessica is dressed in a royal blue top that highlights her blue eyes. On her lap is a cardboard box full of letters. Ashley has on a coral top with lace embroidering on it. She nervously picks at the lace on the cuff of her sleeve as Jessica addresses the audience.

JESSICA
(*smiles*) Hello, America. Earlier today Ash and I found this when we were in the library. (*She shuffles through the box.*) We came across these cards, these letters. They're correspondence from Jane to her mother back home. (*Her eyes tear up.*) We read through each and every letter. They're beautiful. I don't know what they were doing here at the castle. My family should have had them.

ASHLEY
(*stops picking at her sleeve and looks up*) Oh! Don't cry, Jess. You've got them now.

JESSICA
Right. Yes. It's just that I know my mother would have liked to have them.

ASHLEY
Tell America what they say.

JESSICA
*(pulling out a letter from the box and
opening it)* She wanted to go home. She
was afraid here *(shivers)* and I can
understand why.

ASHLEY
(poking Jessica) Don't fall apart now, Jess.
(turning to the camera) America, obviously
Jane was afraid of something. We think that
she may have witnessed something.
Something . . .

JESSICA
Something criminal.

ASHLEY
Yes! Something someone wanted to keep
secret.

JESSICA
Please vote for us. We're so close. If we
had a little more time, we could investigate
further. We've read through every single one
of these letters—

ASHLEY
And I get a strange vibe from everything
we've learned.

JESSICA
(adamantly nods)

ASHLEY
Vote for us.

Twenty

....

"What do you think we'll find in the police report?" Scott asked.

His voice was low and soft as we were outside the library waiting for our turn in front of the camera. Dr. Arch and Karen were up next and I certainly didn't want them to overhear our strategy.

I shrugged, and leaned in close to his ear. "Well, if it's access to Jane's homicide file, we'll find out who they questioned and get access to all the statements."

"What do you mean if it's Jane's file? Who else's file would it be?" he asked.

I smirked. "I'd love access to Merle Greens's file, and the groundskeeper's and Father Gabriel's files."

Scott grinned back at me. "You don't ask for much."

The doors to the library flew open, and Ashley and

Jessica vaulted out of the room. Cheryl motioned Dr. Arch and Karen inside, counting down, "And live in ten, nine, eight . . ."

The doors closed on us and we waited in silence for our turn.

INT. LIBRARY NIGHT

Dr. Arch and Karen are in the same red-striped high-back chairs that Ashley and Jessica have just vacated. Dr. Arch is dressed in a button-down ivory shirt and dress slacks. He tilts his head ever so slightly to the left and stares directly into the camera. Karen makes a show of stretching her long legs out, almost extending into space. She rolls her ankles and lets her red high heel slip off the back of her foot. She dangles the shoe off her toes as she grins into the camera.

DR. ARCH
(*smiles*) Hello, America. We've had a
difficult time investigating the murder of
Jane Reiner—

KAREN
(*patting his knee*) Don't be so hard on
yourself, doctor. The case has gone unsolved
for almost fifty years!

DR. ARCH

(*nods*) Thank you, Karen. (*turning back to the camera*) However, we found a few things that we believe the other teams are unaware of. There's a dumbwaiter that leads from Jane's room into the kitchen.

KAREN

(*wiggling a finger at the camera*) It appears that Jane may have used that dumbwaiter a few times. To escape out of her room after hours. (*tilts her head coquettishly at the doctor*) Now, what girl hasn't wanted to sneak around every now and again?

DR. ARCH

(*looking alarmed, he speaks over Karen*) Yes. Thank you, Karen. (*turns back to the camera*) America! We need more time. We need access to those police reports. Please vote for us. We will make sure that Jane Reiner gets justice.

The doors to the library flew open, and Dr. Arch and Karen spilled out into the hallway.

His hand was on her arm. "Really! What's gotten into you? Did you get into the rum?"

They barreled past us as Cheryl poked her head out the door. "Georgia, please, a personal favor. This is live. For me. Be good."

Before I could reply, she pulled us into the room and thrust us toward some chairs.

"And live in ten, nine, eight . . ."

INT. LIBRARY NIGHT

Georgia and Scott are seated in red-striped high-back chairs. Georgia's hair is pulled back and she looks stunning in a green halter that shows off her strong shoulders. She faces the camera directly with an intense and determined look. Scott has a more relaxed posture. He wears a tight white T-shirt that flatters his muscular chest. His eyes are fixed on Georgia.

GEORGIA
Hello, America. I know you are as anxious as Scott and I are to solve the murder of Jane Reiner, but we need your help. I believe Jane Reiner was killed on the third floor. I would love to get up there and investigate but I've been prohibited. Access has been restricted to us, since I . . . (*She rubs at her leg.*) Since I fell through the floor.

SCOTT
You'd risk life and limb to figure this thing
out, huh, Georgia?

GEORGIA
(shrugs) I don't really think of it that way.
I know I can find justice for Jane. If only
I had access to those police records—

SCOTT
Don't sell yourself short.

GEORGIA
(glances at Scott) What?

SCOTT
You're the smartest person I know. You can
solve this thing. I have complete faith in
you and I know America does, too.

GEORGIA
(blushes and lowers her eyes) Thank you.

SCOTT
(stands up and pulls Georgia to her feet) You
have to believe. I know you don't believe in
all the crazy stuff going on in the castle.
But you have to believe in yourself. In me.
(pauses, takes her face in his hands) In us.

GEORGIA
(takes his hands in hers) I do. Oh, Scott. I
believe in you. I believe in us.

(Scott leans in and kisses Georgia.)

"And cut!" Cheryl screeched, interrupting my delicious moment with Scott. "Fabulous, you two!"

The bright lights from the camera clicked off, leaving us in relative darkness. I blinked rapidly trying to adjust to the change. My knees felt week and I wanted to cling to Scott forever. His arm was around my waist and he whispered, "Everyone is clearing out. We better get going before the spooks get us."

"Do you really believe in spirits?" I asked him.

He shrugged. "I suppose a part of me always did."

"What about us? Do you still believe in us or . . ." I hesitated.

Was it all for the camera?

His jaw tightened and I felt his arm tense under my palm. "Georgia, I've always believed in us."

My heart soared as my hands wrapped around his neck. I pulled his face close to mine and our noses touched. Time seemed to suspend as I looked into his dark eyes, searching for my way home.

Then an unfamiliar voice startled me. "Hmm, guys. Sorry to ruin the moment, but you're standing on my power cord," a technician said.

Scott and I jumped apart and let him wrap up the cord. He smiled wickedly at us. "Anyway, you two probably want to be left in the dark, eh?"

Before we could answer, Becca peeked into the room. She smiled when she saw Scott and me standing so close together. "I'm on babysitting duty tonight. You all have to get to bed now. Cheryl wants to film the elimination as soon as the polls close."

Scott rubbed at his head and moaned. "And what time would that be?"

Becca made a face, ushering us out of the library and down the hall to the main room. "The ungodly hour of five A.M., but hey, I'll have an omelet station and warm coffee waiting for you."

I n the main living room, our sleeping bags were arranged in a semicircle and now with only six of us left, the room seemed eerily quiet.

Scott had fallen asleep almost as soon as his head hit the pillow. And by the sound of Jessica and Ashley's breathing, I figured they were asleep, too. I propped myself up on my elbows to peek at Dr. Arch and Karen Kenley; neither of them moved or seemed to notice me so I supposed they were asleep, too.

Fueled with the hope Scott had given me, I felt wired. I wanted more answers. Crawling out of my sleeping bag, I inched toward the door, flirting with the idea of heading back to the third floor. But my thigh still felt tight and sore, and just the thought of going back up there seemed to make it burn a little.

Once in the hallway, I knew the idea of going upstairs was out of the question. The corridor was pitch black and I had no light. No way would I risk falling again. Instead, I headed out toward the front porch, but when I peeked out the window, I saw Becca and Bert chatting by a rosebush.

Becca was likely in charge of monitoring the votes pouring in from tonight's episode, but judging by her body language, tallying votes was the furthest thing from her mind.

Bert plucked a rose out of the bush and handed it to her.

Becca tilted her head, her auburn hair bouncing up and down as she laughed, clearly enjoying herself.

My heart warmed watching them.

Please, God, let us be lucky in love.

I turned away from them and headed back toward the staircase. Dr. Arch and Karen Kenley had been able to examine the basement early today. I hadn't explored that part of the castle yet, and I knew that's where the boys had their dormitories. Rummaging around a few of the crew's duffel bags that were deserted in the dining room, I found a flashlight.

Armed with the small light, I headed down the treacherous staircase and reached the basement. There was a large, shared shower facility, along with an indoor pool. Flashing my light on the placard on the wall, I realized this was an intake procedure for all the boys. They were dunked in disinfectant upon admission to the school.

I shuddered with horror at the thought.

Proceeding down the corridor, I found another small dormitory. The rooms on the right-hand side of the castle had individual fireplaces, while the rooms on the left-hand side had sinks. I guess it was luck of the draw.

If I could have only one, which would I pick?

I suddenly felt grateful for our modern-day conveniences. A draft rustled through the basement, and I swore I heard a sound from behind me.

I whipped around and flashed the light in the direction of the sound.

Nothing.

Was it just my imagination?

Or was I being followed?

"Scott?" I whispered. When no reply came, I called out, "Dr. Arch? Is that you?"

Only silence answered me, but a strange smell wafted toward me.

Sulfur?

Kerosene?

I recalled Bert saying the smell was evidence of a presence and strained to see anything in the darkness.

I thought about my dream of Jane, and this time, I shined my light, looking around the basement for a floating apparition. I laughed to myself.

Was I starting to believe that ghosts were real?

After another round of examination with my flashlight, I determined there was no one in the basement with me.

Goodness, I was close to losing my mind!

At the end of the corridor, I found something strange, another room. I opened the door, but this room was only five by eight. It had padded walls and there was one small barred window.

Chills crept up my spine.

This must have been the room that they held the boys in during a solitary confinement.

I crossed the room to look out the dirty window. I was facing the front of the castle. The rosebush where Becca and Bert had been earlier was now visible. They were no longer in front of the bush. Where had they gone?

Suddenly, the door slammed.

Oh, my Lord!

What had just happened?

My heart leapt out of my chest as I rushed to the door. I yanked on the knob. It was locked.

I pounded on the door with all my might. "Hey! Hey! Is someone out there? Let me out!"

Was this a sick joke?

Had Dr. Arch followed me again? He seemed to be everywhere I turned, especially if something terrible was about to happen. I pounded on the door again. "Dr. Arch, if that's you, let me out!"

What a creep!

I took a deep breath and reevaluated the room. There was no draft, so the door hadn't blown closed. Someone had definitely locked me in here.

I pounded again.

No answer.

I yanked on the doorknob again, desperate to jimmy it open. I had nothing on me, no hairpin or metal or any device at all to pry it open. I rapped on the door with my flashlight, hoping to create enough of a ruckus to wake someone upstairs.

When I got tired of banging on the door, I returned to the window and rapped on it through the bars. The thing was rock solid. I wondered if I could throw the flashlight or my shoe and break the glass. But then what? It was too small to climb out of, not to mention the bars.

I was stuck.

Twenty-one

....

'd lost track of time wondering if anyone knew that I'd disappeared. Would Scott sleep straight through the night? My flashlight was dimming, now on low battery, and it was getting darker and darker in the cell. I imagined I felt the same emotions one of the boys attending the reform school might have felt.

A complete loss of hope.

Certainly by morning someone would miss me and they'd do a search. Would they find me here in this solitary confinement room? Why hadn't I told anyone where I was going?

Because they would have tried to stop me.

Well, once a rule breaker always a rule breaker, I supposed.

Wasn't that what had got me fired from the SFPD and

started my entire reality TV saga in the first place? I'd been canned for putting the people of San Francisco before the newly appointed police chief, and obviously that's against every political rulebook ever written.

Oh, well, it was no good thinking about my past career. Those negative thoughts would get me nowhere.

Who could have locked me in? Had it been Dr. Arch? Why was he always the first one on the scene when there was trouble?

What happened to Father Gabriel?

If what Dr. Arch said was true and he'd fallowed me upstairs, had someone been up there before us?

Who would want to harm Father Gabriel?

I knew Jessica and Ashley had been in the library with Scott, so they were out. Jack and Martha had left, so they seemed to be cleared of suspicion, too. Although Father Gabriel and Bert had both been released from the show and had stuck around, could the same be true for Martha?

Did she have any reason to want to hurt her own brother?

But then, what about the groundskeeper? What possible motive could anyone have had to hurt him?

And what about the fact that both Father Gabriel and the groundskeeper had attended the school as boys? Obviously, they were connected, but no one else in the cast and crew, besides Martha, was the right age to have attended or worked at the school.

I thought about Jessica; she was the grand-niece of

Jane. Certainly, then, it was possible others were connected to the school even if they hadn't personally attended.

The groundskeeper had been drowned and then his body moved to the pool. How had he been moved? Could Jessica have lifted him? No, it didn't seem possible.

I racked my brain to think of the ground around the pool the day I'd found the groundskeeper dead. It hadn't appeared obvious that anyone had dragged a body across the dirt.

But he hadn't gotten there out of thin air . . . How then?

My brain hurt, and my eyes stung.

I was getting nowhere with my investigation . . .

I must have drifted off, because suddenly there was a rapping at the door.

I jumped up and ran to the door, pounding on it myself. "Help! Help!" I cried.

Then I heard Becca's voice. "Georgia! Are you in there?"

I pressed both my palms and an ear against the door. "Becca?"

"We have to find a key, hold tight," she said. "Okay?" She rapped on the door twice for confirmation.

"Okay," I said, rapping back.

Relief filled me. I'd been found! Soon I'd be out of the small box of a room and breathing fresh air!

After what seemed an eternity, Becca finally returned, only they must not have found a key because a loud splintering, hammering sound shook the door.

An ax!

"Stand back," a loud male voice that I didn't recognize said.

Finally, the door shattered, and a big burly fireman burst through. "Are you all right?" he asked.

Behind him stood Becca, Bert, Cheryl, and Scott. Everyone poured into the room. It was close quarters, but I was so elated to see them that I didn't care.

Scott embraced me, smooching my face. "My God, we were so frightened, we didn't know where you had gone off to."

"How did you find me?" I asked.

Becca said, "Well, that was thanks to Bert."

I looked at Bert and he said, "I got one of my headaches. I knew there was something wrong and we started to look for you, and finally the pain led me here."

I couldn't help the doubt that crept into my stomach. Was he telling the truth? How could he have sensed that I was here?

An awful feeling landed in my gut.

Could it have been Bert who locked me in here in the first place?

Maybe trying to scare me off or something?

We left the room and walked into the basement. All of a sudden the space seemed vast, and I felt more lost than ever.

"I need air," I said to Scott. "Can we go outside?"

"Yes, of course," he said, lacing his fingers through mine. Together we all walked into the courtyard.

Outside, the night was still pitch black, save for the

beautiful country sky and the lights from the fire truck that was parked in front. The back doors of the truck were open with medical equipment spewing out of them. An EMT stood at the ready to give me a cursory evaluation. He took my pulse and my blood pressure. Fortunately, he declared me well, but offered to take me into the hospital for a formal evaluation.

I declined.

When the fire fighter and EMT left, Cheryl grabbed my wrist. "I'm so glad that we found you. The place will be crawling with attorneys in the morning and I need your help."

"How can I help?" I asked.

"Well, we have to convince Gertrude to get off our case. She was livid. Called me at the Indian casino. She can't believe we haven't left the premises yet." Cheryl shook her head. "Pfft. As if I'd leave before we've finished filming."

"How can I help?" I asked again.

Cheryl got a stern look on her face. "Number one, we need to finish filming the show before Lowenstein returns. I wanted Mr. Martin to hash something out with him, but he can only buy us so much time. I need everybody in hair and makeup as early as possible." She glanced at her watch. "It's already four A.M. I need you to get in there at five A.M."

"Oh, no," I moaned.

She patted my shoulder. "Don't worry, Kyle can do wonders."

Becca examined my face. "I think he can probably even hide the bags under your eyes."

"Geez, thanks," I said, shooing her away. I turned to Cheryl. "I think it's time we acknowledged the fact that there's been two murders since we've been here and this property isn't exactly safe. I mean somebody locked me in that solitary confinement cell." I glared at Bert.

His face paled and he took a step away from me. "I hope you're not accusing me of that." he said.

"How else would you know I was there?" I fired back at him.

Becca got between us. "No, no! What are you saying, Georgia? It wasn't Bert. He wouldn't do that." She glanced at him nervously. "Anyway, what time did it happen? How long have you been in there?"

I admitted to seeing them together near the rosebushes, and Becca grabbed Bert's hand possessively.

"It's okay, she's just tired," Scott said, putting a protective arm around me. "Let's go inside and at least let her have an hour's rest before we have to get to hair and makeup."

"Rest?" Cheryl squawked. "She should have rested when she landed herself in solitary confinement. Pump her with coffee."

Scott gave her a nasty look, but before he could say anything else, she added, "Oh, and in case your memory is failing: Third floor is off limits, staircase is off limits, dumbwaiter is off limits." Cheryl said this in my face.

"All right, all right. I know. You don't have to get in my face about it," I whined.

"Apparently I do," she retorted. "Not that you listen."

It was about as much as I could take. Worn down by fatigue, anger suddenly flared inside me, my blood boiling. I got right back in her face. "Like you listen to Mr. Lowenstein and—"

Scott snaked an arm around my waist and pulled me away from Cheryl. "Arguing isn't going to help, ladies." He turned to me. "You shouldn't have gone off by yourself, Georgia," Scott said, lowering his voice. "These people are crazy. Dr. Arch and Karen think that you did something with the votes and this was your cover."

"What?" My blood went cold. I didn't know how to answer that. "Of course I didn't do anything like that," I stuttered.

Suddenly I felt alone. I glanced around the room, noticing for the first time that my father was nowhere in sight. "Where's my dad?" I asked Cheryl. I needed a strong ally on my side. After all, Becca seemed to be on Bert's side and Scott, I didn't know which way he was turning these days.

Cheryl said, "Your father's returned to the farm. The sheriff had a lead on the carjacker. He doesn't know that you were missing. I haven't called him, because I didn't want to alarm him." She shot me a sour look. "Knowing you, I figured you'd show up sooner or later."

I ignored her snide comment and decided to be grateful she hadn't worried dad. My father had been under so much stress, he didn't need to be preoccupied with me right now.

Now, if only I could figure out who'd locked me in the cell.

Rest out of the question, the cast was awake and on edge and Kyle seemed to have started to put together a makeup corner. It looked like the paranormal docent, Ashley, and Jessica were taking turns under his doting attention. I turned to Scott. "Maybe we can solve this thing and be done early."

"Sure," he said, "that would be nice. We could get out of here and get back to normal life." Hope flooded through my belly. Did he mean normal life with me? Would things ever be normal between us again?

Before he could say anything else, Dr. Arch approached us. "Oh, Georgia, I'm glad you've been found. You gave us quite a scare."

"I'm sure you were shaking in your boots," I spit.

He frowned. "What's that supposed to mean?"

I said, "I have a strong suspicion that it might have been you that trapped me in the cell in the first place."

He looked offended.

Karen Kenley appeared and wrapped herself on his arm. "Oh, Georgia, I'm glad everything's all right. Where were you?" she asked, as if she didn't know.

I tried to keep the malice out of my voice, when I demanded, "Where were you all at say ten thirty P.M.?"

They glanced at each other. "We were up here, where the cast was. Asleep, I might add," Karen said. "Until that awful racket. Why would you wander off?"

"Unless you have information we don't," Dr. Arch said, glaring at me.

"What's the dirty look for?" I asked.

Dr. Arch tapped his foot. "Well that's what I'm wondering. Do you have special access to different areas of the castle? If so, this is unfair . . . You have an unfair advantage. You've been sneaking off when we've all been together. I think that calls for an immediate expulsion," he declared.

Cheryl was rushing around ignoring him. "Everybody get into hair and makeup. We'll be filming the next scene soon. After this elimination it's down to the final four."

Dr. Arch pointed a finger and made a melodramatic statement: "Georgia and Scott should be eliminated from the show right now. They have been tampering with the rules."

Cheryl said, "Don't be ridiculous."

"How do you explain that she's been off investigating the castle on her own?"

Cheryl gave Dr. Arch an irritated glare. "Listen, we need to get on with production as quickly as possible before we get expelled from the castle, so I need you to, you know, act professional."

"How do we know Georgia didn't sneak off to meddle with the voting results?" Karen Kenley said. She stood with both hands on her hips and her feet shoulder-width apart, in a sort of Wonder Woman pose, blocking Cheryl from bustling past her.

Cheryl did the only thing a self-appointed king of the jungle would do. She let out a ferocious roar and threw her hands in the air. The entire room went silent and Karen retreated immediately.

Cheryl's gaze rounded the room, taking in every single person. "Anyone want to resign? Right now, you have your chance. Just raise your hand and I'll get your check ready."

I glanced at Scott. I was ready to resign, my hand itched to go up, but instead Scott took it and pressed my fingers to his lips.

"All right then!" Cheryl said. "Let's get back to work!"

"I need a heater in here," Kyle whined. "My hands are so cold I can't work."

Cheryl gave him an icy stare that should have frozen his mouth shut, but he only shrugged and added, "At least I'm not begging for a margarita machine."

Despite her suit of armor, Cheryl softened and a smile cracked through. She studied Kyle, who was dressed in jeans and had a fluffy white winter coat on. "You look like the Polar Bear Express."

Kyle stiffened. "If it wasn't like Antarctica in here, I wouldn't have to dress like this."

Scott clapped his hands together. "Actually, I was hoping I could get one of those," he joked trying to make light of the situation.

Kyle bristled. "With your shaved head, I'm afraid you'd look like the Stay Puft Marshmallow Man."

Scott laughed and rubbed at his head, taking no offense to the gibe.

"All right," Cheryl muttered. "Someone dig out a space heater for our diva over here."

A techie with a green and purple Mohawk raced out of the room. Cheryl glanced at her wristwatch and took off after the techie, mumbling something about checking the results. Soon, the crew member with the Mohawk returned with a portable heater fan. He plugged it in the center of the room and the cast huddled around it, as if it were a campfire.

"Anyone up for some s'mores?" Jessica joked.

Becca paced the room, madly punching buttons on her cell phone. Bert followed her around the room like a very big red puppy dog. Every time she looked annoyed with her phone, he scratched at his beard and frowned.

"Where is the caterer? We need our omelet station and coffee bar!" Becca said. She turned to Bert and said something to him that I couldn't hear, but he nodded and happily left the room

"Mmm, omelet station," Jessica said. "The meals here were awful until she arrived."

Kyle shuffled us around, dragging me over to the makeup chair. "I'm going minimal, darling. Cheryl wants everyone to look run-down. Like you all are working overtime on the case."

I laughed. "Is that retaliation for everyone's bad behavior?"

Kyle shrugged, grabbing the straightening iron. "I just do as I'm told." He took a strand of my hair and placed it in the flat iron, working the strand until it had an amazing glossy look. Despite his instruction, by the time he was done with me, I was sure no one would ever guess I'd spent the night in solitary confinement.

"I'll bet," I said, glancing around the room. "I'm sure you'll get an earful from Dr. Arch." I realized that he wasn't in sight, and neither was Karen.

Now where had they gone off to?

"What's that burning smell?" Ashley asked.

Kyle shrieked. "OMG, am I burning your hair?"

Scott looked from Kyle to me. "No, I don't think it's that—"

As we all turned to look at the heater, it all of a sudden spontaneously combusted and shot itself into a ball of flames.

The group let out a collective scream and everyone scampered around the room.

"Holy Christ," Scott yelled. "Where's a fire extinguisher?"

"Call 911," Jessica yelled.

"Get back!" Becca cried.

"Let me out of here," Ashley screamed, running out of the room and into the hallway.

Most everyone shot out of the room after her, leaving only Scott, Kyle, Becca, and me.

Scott raced to unplug the heater as I frantically looked around the room. The castle obviously wasn't up to fire safety standards; there was no fire extinguisher at hand.

"Give me your coat," I said to Kyle.

He looked horrified. "What?"

"We need to snuff it out before the floor catches!" I shouted. "Come on." As dry and rotten as the wooden floor was, if one ember caught we'd be standing in ashes.

Kyle begrudgingly shrugged out of his coat and handed it to me.

I threw his coat over the fan; it immediately turned into a fireball and knocked the fan over. The dry wood underneath caught fire.

"Holy smokes!" I yelled. "We need to back up. Everyone out!"

Bert raced into the room with a First Alert Tundra fire extinguisher. It was no bigger than a can of aerosol hair spray, but once Bert released the stream of fire-squelching chemicals it immediately covered the scorched wood and heater, tamping the fire out.

Cheryl ran in after him, screaming, "What's going on! What's happened?"

Becca grabbed her arm. "This place is totally haunted, or cursed or whatever." She pointed at the heater. "That thing just spontaneously combusted."

Cheryl buried her face in her hands. "Will this show ever be over? Now I'll have to deal with Gertrude on smoke damage and burn marks." She whipped around and stared at me. "Was this you?"

"I was nowhere near it! I swear," I exclaimed in my defense.

"I'm telling you, I think it's a ghost. I'm a believer now," Becca said, clinging to Bert's arm.

Bert shook his head. "I don't think so. Something's not right. It doesn't smell like a specter to me."

"It's smells like smoke," Cheryl said, sarcastically.

"It's not that," Scott said. "When I pulled the plug from the wall, I got a shock. I think someone tampered with it."

"Why would anyone do that?" Cheryl asked.

I glanced around the room, something nagging at me. "Hey, where did Dr. Arch and Karen Kenley disappear to? They were gone when the thing burst into flames."

Scott quirked his head to the side. "You think Dr. Arch is an arsonist?"

"He's something," I said.

And I'm going to figure out what.

Twenty-two

·····································

While the smoke cleared from the main living room, Cheryl assembled us into the parlor for the elimination scene. As soon as I saw Dr. Arch, I beelined toward him.

"And where have you been?" I demanded. "We had an emergency in the other room and I noticed you and your cohort had conveniently disappeared."

He stared at me. "I don't believe I'm under any obligation to discuss my whereabouts with you."

I ignored him and flipped around to Karen. "I suppose sabotaging a heater is within your FBI-trained skills."

She batted her eyelash extensions at me. "I'm sure I don't know what you mean."

"All right, save the detecting for the camera," Cheryl

said, striding between us. "I have an elimination scene to film."

Harris entered the room, with a paper cup of coffee in one hand and three envelopes in the other. He wore a scowl on his face that said all too clearly he didn't like early morning shoots. But ever the professional, on Cheryl's cue, he handed off his cup to one of the crew members, then flashed his over-whitened teeth and clicked his snakeskin Berluti loafers together to get the audience's attention.

"Hello, America!" he cooed. "Welcome back to *Cold Case in the Castle*! Where we're getting closer to solving the murder of Jane Reiner. As you know, the competition is stiff here, but we can only have one winner. Last night we asked you to decide who should stay and investigate further and who should be eliminated. Well, America, you've spoken!" He tapped the envelopes he held in his hand. "I've been told that we broke records last night with all the viewers phoning, texting, and tweeting." He covered his heart with his free hand. "We here at RTV Studios thank you from the bottom of our hearts for all your support. Now the votes have been tallied and, unfortunately, it's time to say good-bye to one of our favorite contestants."

He tore open the first envelope and nodded as he read it. "Dr. Arch, Karen, you'll be happy to know that your fans regard you as the best in the business. You are safe from this elimination."

Dr. Arch drew a breath, and flashed me an arrogant look.

I said nothing. I'd always figured it would be Scott and me against Dr. Arch and Karen in the end.

Jessica and Ashley fidgeted next to us. Ashley repeatedly rocked back and forth on her heels, while Jessica continued to twirl a lock of her blond hair around and around on her finger.

Scott put his arm around me and pulled me close. The heat from his body calmed my nerves as Harris tore open the next envelope. He frowned for a moment and looked up. "Is this right?"

"Keep rolling!" Cheryl said. "Just read the card, Harris."

Harris nodded and called out, "Jessica and Ashley . . ."

My breath caught.

Could it be that Scott and I would be eliminated?

"I'm pleased to tell you that you are safe from elimination," Harris finished.

A hush came over the room, as if the oxygen had been sucked out of it.

Ashley suddenly gasped. "What?"

Jessica grabbed my hand. "Oh, no! No, no!"

Ashley thumped Scott on the back. "Sorry to see you go! But hey, I'm glad it's not us."

My brain was slow to compute what was happening. Scott and I were off the show? Was that right?

Harris said, "Georgia, Scott, unfortunately, I'm sorry

to say you will not be solving this mystery this time." He clapped his hands and said, "Now it's time for you to say your good-byes."

We've been voted off.

"We didn't make the final four," I mumbled.

Scott shook hands with Harris, then with Dr. Arch. Dr. Arch was looking rather smug and part of me was relieved to say good-bye to him.

But the other part of me was fuming. I had fully invested myself in figuring out what had happened to Jane. I had stitches on my leg to prove my dedication and yet it hadn't seemed to matter in the end.

Scott put an arm around my shoulder and ushered me out of the room.

"I can't believe it's over," I said as we walked down the corridor toward the front door of the castle.

He shrugged. "Well, I find it hard to believe that America would vote for Dr. Arch over you. But I can say, I probably wasn't the best teammate."

"No! Don't say that." I stopped and grabbed his shoulder. "You're a great teammate, Scott. I love you."

The sound of rustling behind us interrupted us. We turned to see Becca and Bert charging at us. "Georgia! What's going on?" she asked. "What's happened? What are you two doing out here?"

I shrugged. "What do you mean? We're off the show."

"What?" Shock distorted her sweet features and she shook her head in disbelief. "How can that be?"

"I guess America voted," Bert said. "It's hard to believe,

because you were such a shoo-in, but we can't ever take anything for granted. I took the elimination pretty hard, too, but I'm okay with the consolation prize." He put an arm around Becca and crushed her to his side.

She squealed with delight, and my heart filled with joy for her. I so wanted her to find a perfect match.

Scott turned to Bert. "Did you have any idea that we would be eliminated? I mean, did you get a vision or whatever?"

Bert shook his head. "No. I don't get them all the time. In fact, usually not as frequent as lately. I think something about the castle was really fueling my abilities."

"The place really is haunted," Becca said. "All the stuff going down can't be a coincidence."

"Oh, come on," I said. "Everything has an explanation. The blackbirds were migrating, the floor was rotten through, and the heater was tampered with."

"What about you being locked in the cell last night?" Scott asked.

I shrugged. "I'm going to account for everything. I don't care if they voted me off or not. I'm going to figure out who murdered Jane, the groundskeeper, and Father Gabriel. And I'll bet whoever killed the last two was probably the person who locked me in the cell."

Becca hugged me. "That's the spirit. That's what I love about you, and that's what the producer of *Globe Tracker* will love, too."

My mouth went dry as disappointment choked me. "Do you think that they'll still want me?"

She patted my shoulder. "I don't know, honey. It's hard to say, but I'll reach out to them. It'll be my first call."

"What are you talking about?" Scott asked, and when I turned to look at him, I was shocked to see he'd paled.

Becca pressed her lips together and gave us a fleeting glance. "Oops. Bert, we should see if Cheryl needs us."

Bert wiggled his fingers at me as he and Becca took off down the dark corridor.

Scott flung open the front door of the castle and stormed out.

"Wait!" I called after him. "Scott! Let me explain."

The sun was coming up in the east, casting a warm glow on the Golden Castle and I desperately wished I could feel that warmth in my heart. Instead, all I felt was dread.

Scott stopped short of the wooden steps, and turned to look at me. His face was stoic. "Go ahead. Explain. When were you going tell me?"

I shrugged. "I . . . I don't know. There's not really anything to tell. I don't even know if it's happening."

"But we're a couple, right? We're supposed to tell each other these things. Communication, Georgia! It's pretty obvious," he said.

Anxiety bubbled up inside me. "You said you needed space. I was trying not to confuse things."

"Well, needing space and not telling me what's going on with you are two different things."

"They are?" I asked.

"Yes!" he said. "You don't even trust me enough to tell

me that you have an offer? What? Are you supposed to move to L.A. now?"

"I don't know," I said. "I don't really have any information, and it's not an offer."

"But it's been ongoing," he said. "And you haven't told me anything."

"I'm sorry," I said. "I didn't know if it was important."

"Well, of course it's important. I mean . . ." He stopped talking suddenly and buried his head in his hands.

Despair clawed at me.

How could I have messed things up with Scott?

I reached out for him, but he stepped away from me, avoiding my reach. "Scott, it doesn't mean anything. Becca and I were just chatting, you know? If it had turned into anything real, I would have told you."

"Told me, huh? Informed me." He folded his arms across his chest, cutting himself off from me.

"I don't mean it like that," I said.

"Yes, you do. You would have told me your decision, meaning I have no part in the decision making."

I felt completely deflated and tears threatened. "Scott," I pleaded. "I need to work. I need to have an income. You know that."

His face softened as he looked at me, seemingly judging my sincerity. "I know. But if we were planning to get married, wouldn't my income be enough for us?"

My throat ached from holding back tears, yet I managed to whisper, "I've never expected a man to support me."

"So what does that mean? You marry a man and just take off to L.A.?"

"Marry you? I didn't know . . ."

"You didn't know I was getting ready to propose?" he asked.

My knees felt weak.

I'd screwed everything up.

All this time I'd been fretting over Scott's feeling for me and yet what had I done? I'd managed to make plans that didn't include him. Was that some kind of stupid defense mechanism?

Was I sabotaging myself? Pushing away the only thing I ever really wanted. To be loved. To marry. To have a family.

And for what?

To be on reality TV?

My stomach lurched and I fought the nausea that rumbled in my belly.

"How could I have known?" I sputtered. "You said you wanted space. You said you weren't sure if you loved me. And now you tell me you were getting ready to propose? I don't understand!"

"Well, I wanted space to sort things out," Scott said. "I was numb for a long time, and I just didn't really know what I was feeling. I was confused.. But I thought we were . . . I thought that the track we were on, a life together . . ."

My heart constricted, and I resisted throwing myself into his arms. "Yes! Yes! It's the track we were on."

He sighed. "Well, if it's the track we were on, how do you expect to live a life with somebody when you go to a different town for work?"

"I don't know," I croaked, my voice cracking with emotion. "I hadn't thought it through."

"Because I'm not a priority," he said, and I noticed for the first time that the edges of his eyes were turning red. He wiped at them angrily.

I grabbed his hands. "Scott! Scott! It's not that. I promise—"

He pulled his hands out of mine, a small noise escaping his throat. "Maybe we do need a break, Georgia."

My heart clenched, my breath catching.

This was it.

This was the moment that I had feared.

"No, Scott! No," I stammered. "We're not ready for a break. I love you."

He pressed his lips together, and rubbed at his face. "Are you sure about that, Georgia?"

His words hit me like a cannonball in the stomach.

He was right.

Even though I knew he'd been having a hard time these past few days, I hadn't done anything to make it easier for him. Maybe it was me. Maybe I was the one who was scared of commitment.

Tears bubbled up, and I ran at him and hugged him. "No, we're not ready for a break, Scott. I love you," I said.

He hugged me back, stiffly, patting my shoulder in a

very cold, platonic way. "You'll get over me, Georgia. I think you're practically over me anyway," he said.

Before I could protest further, he released me and rushed away.

I was left alone, feeling the warmth of the rising sun on my skin, wishing I could die.

Twenty-three

....

After Scott left, I sat on the front porch awhile, wallowing in self-pity. I wept until the tears stopped coming, leaving me feeling weak and hopeless.

Finally, I decided that the only good thing about being let off the show was that it would give me free rein to investigate, and I definitely needed an investigation to get my mind off my disastrous love life.

I retrieved my phone from one of the crew members and borrowed Becca's car to drive into town. I hadn't eaten breakfast, so I stopped into the local bakery, Golden Confections, and fortified myself with chocolate-banana grilled cinnamon toast. It was so delicious it almost made things right with the world. Until I licked the bit of powdered sugar from my fingers and remembered Scott.

A dry sob escaped me, and the girl behind the counter

wearing tricolor wood plug earrings quirked a heavily studded eyebrow at me. "Everything okay?" she asked.

"Peachy," I said. "How about two dozen donuts?"

"Suit yourself." She shrugged, popping the sugary delights into a pink pastry box.

I paid and left, headed toward the local police station. I didn't know anything if I didn't know cops. Outside the station, I parked and dug around Becca's glove box. Finding a salmon-colored lip gloss, I applied it liberally. It wasn't really my color, but it was better than nothing. And at least it mildly distracted an onlooker from the fact that I'd been bawling my eyes out for the past three hours.

I got out of the car and clutched the pink pastry box for moral support. At the door of the police station I had to balance the box on my hip, while I pushed open the heavy door. Inside it was institutional and sparse. Two uniformed officers sat at computer stations. One, a woman, was wearing a headset and had an angry expression on her face. The other, a bald man, sat with a bored look, undoubtedly surfing Facebook for some excitement.

As soon as I walked in, he perked up and eyed the box.

"Can I help you?" he asked.

I gave him my best nonthreatening, made-for-reality-TV smile. "I'm here to see Officer Holtz."

He frowned, still eyeing the pink pastry box. "I think he's busy. Are these for . . . ?" He let the question dangle.

"Yes. For Officer Holtz," I said. "And whomever may be in the good graces of Officer Holtz."

The woman officer who was wearing the headset made

a face, as if she didn't approve of my bribing the bald officer, but she seemed too preoccupied with her phone call to interfere.

The bald officer's name tag read *Gallagher*. He smiled at me. "Well, I'm in his good graces."

"Of course you are, Officer Gallagher," I said, opening the box. The smell of freshly baked donuts travels fast in a police station. Before long a flock of police officers was chomping down on donuts, and I'd been promptly escorted back to Officer Holtz's desk.

"How did you know cinnamon twist is my favorite?" he asked, wiping the sugar from the corners of his mouth.

"Women's intuition," I replied.

"Which murder most interests you?" he asked.

"All of them," I said. "They have to be interconnected, don't they?"

"Yeah. Unfortunately. I think so." He tapped a pen on his notebook. "I can't wait until they close that castle down, one hazard after another."

"What do you know about Father Gabriel's death?" I asked.

His lips turned into a thin line as if he was deciding how much to share with me. I glanced down at what remained in the pink pastry box. One last cinnamon twist. I pushed it toward him. "I won't tell the wife you broke your diet."

He smiled and happily picked up the twist. "I'm sorry to say I don't have much on the priest. The autopsy reports show he died from the fall. No surprise."

"May I see the file?"

He put the twist down on a napkin and yanked open his file folder. "There's not much in it, but seeing as you've been so hospitable and you were never a suspect . . ."

From inside my jacket, my cell phone buzzed. But there was no way I'd interrupt access to insider information by taking a call at the most inopportune time. I slipped my hand into my pocket and silenced my phone.

Officer Holtz handed me the file, and I perused it slowly. There were photos of Father Gabriel and the surrounding area: the rosebushes, a discarded wheelbarrow, and a muddy patch of ground. Then there were the autopsy photos. After flipping through the photographs, I read through the statements the cast and crew had given. There was nothing to note, really, except that Dr. Arch claimed he'd hurt his hand in the basement when he slipped.

It wasn't unlikely that he'd fallwn in the basement, it'd been so dark, but it seemed too easy an excuse to explain away the injury.

I tapped on the folder. "Dr. Arch. His hand. Could he have hurt it in a squabble with Father Gabriel, like say when he pushed him out the third-floor window?"

Officer Holtz smiled. "I thought the same thing myself, but I saw camera footage of Dr. Arch slipping in the basement. He landed directly on his hand. I'll say at least that piece is true."

Ugh.

"Could the slip be fake?" I asked.

Officer Holtz shrugged. "It looked real enough to me and the cameraman confirmed it."

I tapped on the file again. I had the nagging feeling I was missing something. I flipped through the photos once more.

"The wheelbarrow. What was it doing there?" I asked.

"Hmmm?" Officer Holtz asked. "What do you mean?"

"Thinking out loud here," I said. "The groundskeeper is dead . . . who put the wheelbarrow there near the rosebushes?"

Officer Holtz scratched at his chin and then took a final bite of the cinnamon twist. "I don't know. Does it matter?"

An image came to me of the dirt near the pool. When I'd found the groundskeeper there'd been grooves in the earth that I hadn't been able to identify. Now looking at the photo of the wheelbarrow, I realized the grooves must have come from the wheels on the wheelbarrow.

Why would someone wheel a wheelbarrow up to the edge of an empty dilapidated pool?

I slammed my hand down on his desk suddenly. "That's how the killer transported the body."

"A wheelbarrow?" Holtz asked.

"Exactly! We know the groundskeeper was killed somewhere else and then dumped in the pool. I think the killer wanted to move Father Gabriel's body, too, but I found him and interrupted him."

Holtz shook his head. "I don't get it. Why put the

groundskeeper in the pool? Why kill the priest? None of it makes any sense."

"Will you loan me Jane Reiner's file?" I asked.

He nodded. "Sure, that one is public. In fact, I made a copy of it recently for your show." He dug around his desk and handed me a thick file with yellowing papers. "Have at it."

I stood, then hesitated. "Oh, Officer Holtz. Do you have the file on Merle Greens?"

Holtz frowned. "Merle Greens? Who is that?"

"He drowned in the river a few weeks before Jane was murdered."

Holtz nodded. "I'll get it for you, but it's in archives. It's going take a while."

With Jane's file burning a hole on the passenger side seat of Becca's car, I hightailed it over to the Indian casino and resort and booked myself a room. I figured, as long as I was single and down in the dumps, I may as well treat myself to room service and cry in bed over Scott. Not to mention, I was utterly exhausted after spending the night on the cold floor of the solitary confinement cell.

Once inside the room I read through the police report, then crawled under the awful floral print bedspread and closed my burning eyes.

Not long after I dozed off, there was a knock on the door.

"Georgia, are you in there?" a familiar voice called out.

"Jessica?" I asked, rolling out of bed and padding toward the door.

When I unlocked the door, I found Jessica standing together with Ashley.

"You found me." I said.

Ashley shrugged. "It's the only major hotel in town."

Jessica grabbed my hands. "We need to talk to you."

"Come in," I said. The police report I'd been perusing was spewed out across the desk. Ashley noticed it first.

"You've been investigating?" she asked.

"Yup," I said.

"That's why we came," Jessica said.

"What is it? What's going on?" I asked.

"We want to give you our spot on the show," Jessica said. "I think you're the only one who can solve my great-aunt's murder. We need you there, we have no faith in Dr. Arch and Karen Kenley, they're completely cheating."

"Uh . . . I'm not sure how that would work," I said. "Scott and I, we're not even together anymore." A hollowness bore into my heart as I said the words out loud.

"He's already agreed to come back." Jessica beamed.

Unexpectedly, jealousy jabbed at me. She'd spoken to him? He'd agreed to come back. To what? To see her? To see me?

"I don't know," I hemmed. "I was just trying to get some traction here with the files."

"We've looked at them, too," Ashley said. "There's definitely something going on."

"Father Gabriel was a student at the school," Jessica

said. "He was one of the people who testified about my aunt's murder."

"I saw that," I said. A disquieting feeling overwhelmed me. Something was going on that I needed to get to the bottom of, but I didn't see how going back on the show with its constraints could help me. Ashley took a seat by the window.

"Your friend, Becca, told us about your offer."

"What offer?" I asked.

"The one from Hollywood, where you get to be on the show," Jessica said.

"It would help if you were on *Cold Case in the Castle* and you won," Ashley finished.

I shrugged. "I don't know if it really matters anymore," I said.

"It does and we're not going to beat Dr. Arch and Karen," Jessica said. "As much as I want to get to the bottom of what happened to my aunt, they're not going to let us; they're going to sabotage us every step of the way—" As Jessica was speaking my phone buzzed.

I looked at the caller ID; it was Becca. I looked back at Jessica and Ashley.

"Becca's going to try to convince me to come on the show?" I asked.

They nodded.

"She's been calling you for hours. There's something else you don't know. Becca is sure that someone tampered with the results from last night's show."

"Tampered? What do you mean?" I asked. Without

giving them a chance to reply, I answered my phone and heard Becca scream into my ear.

"Well, are you coming back or what?"

I laughed. "Or what."

"Have you talked to Ashley and Jessica?" she said.

"They're here in my hotel room," I answered.

"Well come on back. Scott's already here and he's chomping at the bit to see you."

I didn't know how to process the news.

Scott wanted to see me again?

It seemed unlikely the way we had parted. Nerves flooded my stomach.

"I've been to the police station. I have the police files," I said.

"That's all right," Becca said. "Bring them with you. We need to have resolution or this is going to be a terrible ending to the show."

I watched as Jessica and Ashley danced around the room, packing up my belongings. Ashley tossed toiletries into my makeup bag, and Jessica was busy emptying drawers into my suitcase. "Guys!" I said, holding up a hand. "I haven't even agreed to anything yet."

"Well, agree already then," Becca said, through the phone.

"All right," I said, hanging up.

"Come on, come on," Jessica said.

"When Dr. Arch finds out, he's going to flip a gasket and I want to be there to watch," Ashley said.

Ah. A woman after my own heart.

Twenty-four

....

When I returned to the castle, Becca and Scott were there to greet me. Scott wrapped his arms around me.

"I think I made a mistake," he said.

"It's all right," I said. "I understand that you need time."

"No," he said. "You don't understand."

He pulled me close to a bench and we sat. Becca made herself scarce.

"All this time, Georgia, I've been trying to remember feeling in love with you, but what's happened through the course of this week is I've fallen in love with you again. I can't explain why I don't remember the past in the way that I want to, but I know what I'm feeling now and I know what I've put you through."

My throat constricted and my mouth went dry. "Are you saying you want to stay with me?" I asked him.

He took my face in his hands. "I'm saying I want you and only you. I know that for sure now. Are you okay with that? And are you okay with me not remembering everything about our past?"

I grabbed his hands. "Yes, I am. I love you, Scott."

He pressed his forehead to mine, our noses touching. "I must know you better than I think because I knew you'd say that."

He smiled his irresistible smile and pressed his lips to mine. Excitement shot through my fingertips as I wrapped my arms around his neck and pressed him close to me.

"All right, you two lovebirds, break it up," Cheryl said as she approached, the gravel crunching under her feet. "We're going to make a big show of Jessica and Ashley picking you guys to take their place."

I groaned. "Might as well get into hair and makeup."

We all walked together back toward the castle, Scott's hand in mine. Kyle was ready to do my hair, this time taking out his curling iron and wielding it with such precision it was alarming.

"I'm glad you're back, doll." he said. "I'm going to make you look extra pretty because I missed you so much."

"You can't have missed me that much. I've only been gone a few hours," I said.

He pulled the curling iron out of my hair, deftly leaving a curl behind. "Oh, well, it must be the guilt then."

257

"Guilt? About what?"

"Don't you remember that I'm the one who sent you up to the third floor? It's my fault you've been limping all this time."

"I'm not limping," I said.

"Sure you are, and I can only give you flat-heeled shoes not comfy sneakers because Cheryl said so." He looked resentful.

"It's not your fault that I'm hurt," I said.

He unplugged the curling iron and wrapped the cord around the base of it. "You forgive me?"

I stood and hugged him. "A girl must never ever be angry with her stylist."

"Lights, camera, action," Cheryl called.

Jessica and Ashley sat across from Scott and me in the library and made a formal presentation to us of the network card and the police reports. Jessica gave a teary speech about her belief that Scott and I were the best team to resolve the murder of her great-aunt. Meanwhile, in the neighboring room Dr. Arch and Karen Kenley fumed.

Once the transition happened, we were given free rein to investigate as long as we kept our cameraman in tow.

"Let's go back to the kitchen," I said to Scott. "Where the dumbwaiter is."

Scott agreed and walked with me to the kitchen. I reexamined the place and I got into the dumbwaiter.

"Do you think you could hoist it to the third floor?" I asked him.

He looked dumbfounded. "What do you mean, G? No, we're not supposed to do that."

I shrugged. "I never follow the rules. You should know this if you're falling in love with me again."

"I can't let you up there." He pulled me out of the dumbwaiter and got in himself. "You hoist me."

I laughed. "There's no way I'll be able to lift you."

"Try," he said. "These things have some leverage in them."

I gave it one heavy pull and lifted him about two inches before releasing the cord and dropping him back with a thud.

He laughed. "Oh, my gosh. And here I thought you were strong."

"I am strong," I said, flexing my bicep.

"Is it me?" he asked, rubbing his flat belly.

"Get out of the box," I said.

He climbed out and I stuffed myself into the dumbwaiter. He began to hoist me up. As the dumbwaiter ascended, I could no longer see Scott.

"Can you hear me?" I asked as I was raised up.

"Yes," he said.

Our cameraman grunted. I knew he was upset that he'd no longer be able to film me, but he dutifully filmed Scott as Scott continued to lift me up. Probably not the most exciting TV. Maybe Scott would sing to liven things up.

"I'm on the first floor now," I said. "Keep going." The box stopped for a few minutes. "Do you need a break?" I asked.

"Uh-huh," I heard from below. I climbed out onto the second floor.

"Just one more floor," I called down.

"Okay. I'll let you know when I'm ready."

After a minute or two Scott called, "Okay, get in, Georgia."

I got into the dumbwaiter and he hoisted me up to the third floor. I got out gingerly.

"All right," I said once there. I examined the room. I was in a corridor. To the left were rooms that I figured might have been Jane's. I walked into one of the rooms, carefully avoiding any wood planks that looked rotted.

From the third floor I could see the river. It had been a heavy water year, raining almost every night. The riverbanks were flooded; any more water and we'd lose a levy. As I stared out to the water I thought about Merle Greens's drowning. He was the first victim. Three weeks prior to Jane's murder. Was there a connection?

I fingered the wood board, the wood trim around the window. Could Jane have seen the accidental drowning from her windowsill?

As I continued to peer out, I saw Gertrude, the head of the historical society, strolling along the gardens. I remembered reading her biography online. She was a local. She'd been a young girl living in Golden at the time Merle had drowned . . .

She was about Jane's age . . .

She'd been living in Golden when Jane had been murdered . . .

She definitely didn't want us here at the castle . . .

Could she have been involved with anyone at the reform school? Could she have had anything to do with Jane's murder?

A chill went up my spine. I had no proof, but I knew nobody wanted us out of the castle more than Gertrude did. I swabbed the inside of the room with the DNA kit that I'd won in the first challenge, and then called down to Scott through the dumbwaiter tunnel.

"Are you ready for me?" I asked.

"I'm here for you, babe."

I climbed back into the box. "Hold it steady now," I said, preparing myself for the bumpy ride. He lowered me down the three flights until I careened into the kitchen and fell out of the dumbwaiter.

I sprawled out on the floor. "Remind me, I don't ever want to do that again."

He picked me up. "I'm sorry."

The cameraman chuckled, happy to get the shot of me falling down onto the kitchen floor.

"Did you find anything?" Scott asked.

I showed him the DNA swab. "Well I've got this, but I don't know how to read it. I think I need to make nice with Karen, the FBI agent."

Scott said, "They're our competition. We're the final four."

261

"I know," I said. "But justice trumps prize money, doesn't it?"

He pulled me close. "Love trumps prize money for sure." He pressed his lips against mine and I felt small shivers of contentment spread through my body.

Twenty-five

....

Scott and I, followed by our cameraman, Adam, made our way down the corridor into the library. Karen looked startled to see us. Dr. Arch quirked an eyebrow as though he had been expecting us.

"What do you say we join forces?" I asked.

Dr. Arch bristled. "Absolutely not."

Karen leaned forward, exhaustion in her eyes. "What do you got?"

"DNA," I said, flashing her my sample.

"Hmm," she said. "I don't know that I can do anything with it. I don't have my regular equipment."

"I understand."

"Where did you get it from?" Dr. Arch asked, trying hard to look indifferent.

"Third floor," I said.

Karen gasped. "I thought the third floor was off limits!"

"It is," Scott said. "Do you want to stop the show?" He quirked an eyebrow at her.

She crossed her arms in front of her chest and said nothing.

Dr. Arch challenged, "What are you implying?"

Scott said, "I think you guys rigged the last round of audience results."

This was news to me. I had no idea that Scott suspected Dr. Arch and Karen of tampering with the results, too, but I decided to play along. Poker-faced, I said, "We have proof."

Karen looked over at me, her eyes growing wide. "What kind of proof?"

Aha. It was the wrong answer. Of course, I had no proof, but she hadn't denied it, either.

Dr. Arch said, "All right. We'll play along. What do you got?"

I gave my DNA findings to Karen.

"I need a microscope," she said.

We looked at the cameraman who looked blankly back at us. "I think we'll have to negotiate that with Cheryl," I said.

"Let's go," she said to Dr. Arch.

"No," Dr. Arch said. "That's what they want. They're sending us on a wild-goose chase while they sit here with the records and buy more time to investigate."

"You don't trust a soul, do you?" Scott asked.

"That's right," Dr. Arch said.

"I'll go with you then," Scott said to Karen. "You and I will track down Cheryl, and Georgia and Dr. Arch will continue to investigate. That way it's fair and square."

Dr. Arch laughed and appraised me like a wolf looks at a lamb. "That'd be fine. Yes. Leave the lovely young woman here with me," he said.

Scott glared at him, but I shooed him away. "I can handle him," I said. "Plus, I got security." I motioned toward the cameraman, who remained fixed in the corner.

"Right," Scott said, kissing my cheek. "Watch him. Don't let him near anything that can blow up."

At that, Dr. Arch made a little smirk and I knew he'd messed with the heater, in order to distract us so he could do God knows what to the voting results.

Sneaky!

Scott and Karen left the room in search of Cheryl, and I took a seat across from Dr. Arch.

"So what have you found? I've looked through the same material over and over again," he said. "I don't know what to make of it." He pointed to a section in the police report about Jane's murder.

I said, "No, you're looking at the wrong information."

"How so?" he asked.

"I think the key is somewhere else." I flipped through the file, searching for any reference to Merle Greens. "Do you know anything about the boy who drowned in the river?" I asked.

Dr. Arch shook his head. "What does that have to do with Jane?"

"I don't know, but there's a view of the river from her room. She wrote to her mother that she'd seen something and I wonder if maybe what she saw was a drowning that was not all that accidental."

"Aha," Dr. Arch said, elongating the vowels in the word the way doctors do.

Together we reviewed the file on Jane again. There had been no eyewitnesses and several children in the school had been questioned, one of whom was young Father Gabriel.

"Did you know he was a student here?" I asked.

Dr. Arch nodded. "He told me as much."

"The day you were on the third floor?" I asked. "Together?"

"Yes," he said.

"Why did you deny being up there?" I asked.

He shrugged. "It was nonsense, really. I'd found the dumbwaiter and followed the path. I found him upstairs. Both of us knew neither of us was supposed to be up there and we certainly didn't want to share anything we'd found. This is a contest after all. Then we heard you break through the floor."

"Did you push him out the window?" I asked.

"Of course not. Don't be ridiculous," Dr. Arch said. "I'm a doctor, not a murderer."

"You'd like to win the show badly," I said. "Your Hollywood career depends on it."

He stared back at me. "Well, so does yours."

"Yes," I said. "I've been invited to be on another show, but the offer's contingent on my doing well here."

He smiled and nodded.

"And you, likewise?" I asked.

He grumbled. "How do you know?"

"It's the way Hollywood works," I said. "Garner an audience, and you get to keep playing."

"Yes," he said, looking a little sad.

"Did you tamper with the results?"

His eyes grew wide, and they flickered over to the camera. "Of course I didn't."

That was all I needed to know. He needed to win this show in order to continue his career, and I needed to get justice.

I flipped through the pages of Jane's file. Something was amiss. Something was missing in this report that was in the file Officer Holtz had given me at the police station.

Gertrude's name was gone.

Someone had scrubbed the report that was given to the final four contestants.

Who would have had access to it? Could Gertrude herself have taken care of that? It suddenly seemed that I needed to speak to Gertrude.

I whipped around to Adam, the cameraman, as I sprang up from my chair. "Tell Cheryl I've got her finale!"

I raced down the corridor and bolted out of the castle in search of Gertrude. In the parking lot was one of the sound techs, whose name I knew was Collin.

I called out to him. "Collin! Collin! Have you seen Gertrude?"

"Who?" he asked.

"The historical society lady, Gertrude. She's running around here, the one who doesn't want us on the third floor who's been trying to kick us out."

"Oh, that bat? Yeah, she just sent our food service truck away. She's hovering around the gardens, but be careful, she's seething. She hates that we're here and can't wait until we're done."

"I need a word with her," I said. Adam, the cameraman, made to follow me but I shooed him away.

"I have to get it on tape," he said. "Every move you make."

"All right," I said, "but not with Gertrude knowing. Can you be discreet?"

He nodded. "I can put a camera on you if you give me a minute."

I agreed. Together we went over to one of the trailers and he set me up with a camera hidden in my clothes. "Is this really going to work?" I asked.

He said, "I don't know, but I think I've set you up a little better than those silly police stings."

I laughed. "Well, what do the cops know? You're a Hollywood pro."

He grinned at me. "Remember, this is not a live feed. Be careful, Georgia."

"Oh, I will be," I said.

After all, I'd been through the police academy. I knew

how to take a suspect down if I needed to. But right now I needed to speak with Gertrude before Scott or Cheryl could stop me.

I headed back toward the gardens and saw that Gertrude was now wandering around the pool grounds.

She saw me approach, her face fixed with a look of disdain. "Are you still skulking around here?"

"I'm not the one skulking," I said. "We have a show to produce."

"Right. Why don't you get back to work? You all are supposed to leave here by ten P.M. tonight. I refuse to let this go on any longer." She glanced at her watch.

"That's exactly what you want, isn't it?" I said. "For us to stop poking around into the murder of Jane Reiner."

She quirked an eyebrow at me. "I want the murderer to be found as much as anyone else."

"Was Jane your friend?" I asked.

She shook her head. "No, no. I didn't know Jane."

"You were living in Golden at the time of her murder. And later you came to work here. You've been at the castle a long time." I said.

"Well, there's nothing unusual about that," she said. "I'm a local. A lot of the locals have been to the castle. We grew up around here."

"But you didn't know Jane?" I asked. "You and she are about the same age."

She looked at me. "No, I wasn't allowed near the castle when I was a youth. There was all sorts of debauchery going on here. My parents wouldn't allow it," she said.

"Right, but you certainly love the castle now. You protect it with everything you have." I said.

She shrugged at me. "So what, a lot of us would. This is our local economy. We make money off the castle. This is how our town survives, otherwise we'd be pushed into the cities with everybody else, living in a bunch of human filing cabinets."

"Apartments?" I asked.

She waved a hand at me. "Call them what you want, but they're certainly not castles. Anyway, working here has allowed me to stay out in the country, enjoy the acreage and the fresh air. There's nothing like it."

She had a point there. Being a farm girl myself, I knew exactly what it was like to live in the country. Instead of arguing with her about the merits of town versus country, I said, "I find it hard to believe that you didn't know Jane."

She jutted her chin out at me, challenging me. "Well, I didn't. Anyway, I've been here all my life. If I had done something suspicious, the police would've caught on by now."

She had a point there, but there was still the problem about the missing page in the police report.

"I saw your name in the police report," I wagered.

She glanced at me. "Yes, I imagine everybody's name was in the police report, the whole town probably," she said. "They asked everybody questions when that poor girl was found."

"Well, the funny thing is, there are pages missing out of the police report the final members of the cast were given." I said.

She looked at me, a blank expression on her face. *Waiting for me to say more.*

"You wouldn't have tampered with something that was given to the contestants, or would you have?" I asked.

Her face turned red and she closed the distance between us. "Listen here. I don't know what you're implying, but I haven't tampered with any police reports. I don't even know what you're talking about," she said.

"Right." I remained calm, itching to increase the distance between us. Because of my training, I knew it was best to keep all her limbs in my line of sight. I took a small step back. "Here's what I think," I said. "I think Jane's murder is connected with the drowning of Merle Greens."

"What? That was an accident," she said. "Everybody knows that. The whole town knows it."

"I'm willing to guess that it wasn't. Somebody drowned him and somebody knew about it. Maybe Jane witnessed it. Could she have been killed to keep her silent and keep the other crime a secret?"

Gertrude looked as if I had completely taken her by surprise. She paled. After a moment, she shrugged. "I don't know. I suppose anything is possible. Stranger things have happened."

I pressed further. "Well, we'll soon know," I said. "I recovered a piece of critical DNA from Jane's bedroom."

She put her hands on her hips. "So you broke the rules again and headed up there, didn't you? I can't wait for all you Hollywood types to be out of here."

"Karen Kenley is investigating the DNA match right now," I said.

Gertrude studied me carefully. "What do you mean?" *Was that fear in her face?*

"We'll soon know the identity of Jane's killer," I bluffed.

Gertrude's eyes shifted around the grounds, looking for an escape. Then our eyes landed on the same item. A rusty pair of pruning shears discarded near the rosebushes.

"We didn't kill Merle," Gertrude said. "He drowned. It was an accident!"

"You were there the day he drowned, weren't you?" I guessed.

"Gabriel was in love with me. He fought with Merle, but it wasn't his fault. Merle slipped on the rocks and smashed his head. We had to get rid of the body or Gabriel would have never been released from the reform school. Walter saw the whole thing. He helped us. We convinced the police that Merle had gone swimming and never returned. And then it was all over," she said.

"But Jane saw the fight, too, right? From her window. You couldn't convince her to stay quiet."

"That's right," Gertrude sneered. "Walter and Gabriel didn't know about her. I knew if they figured out she was a witness, if they knew she could keep them locked up forever, they would have folded. Gabriel was soft and Walter was just stupid. I had to do it."

"All these years—"

"Yes, all these years, I kept it quiet." She shifted

toward the shears, inching closer to them ever so slightly. "Gabriel moved out of state and Walter stayed around, but none of us talked about it. The murder mystery of Jane Reiner kept this castle in business. Haunting tours, Halloween spook-taculars, we were doing all right. Until your stupid Hollywood show came along."

I grimaced. "But the pay was good, right? You thought you could take the money and keep everyone in the dark."

"It would have worked, but after all these years, with you all poking around . . . and seeing Gabriel . . . Walter suddenly developed a conscience, decided he had to confess," she said.

"You couldn't have that."

"No. I killed him in the basement. I would have gotten away with that, too, but you were out by the pool. I thought you saw me. Then Gabriel. He wouldn't leave. I begged him to go, but he returned. I had to get rid of him."

"You were going to use the wheelbarrow again. Move the body."

"Yes," she said. "I had to get rid of the evidence. But you were there again. Everywhere I turn, there you are. It's like you're haunting me."

"That's why you sent me to the third floor, right? Hoping I'd kill myself?"

Her face reddened with fury. "I wish you had. Now I'm going to have to do it myself!"

She dove for the shears, with an agility that astounded me. I raced behind her, slower than I'd anticipated, my stitched thigh tighter than I'd realized.

She reached the shears and hurled them at my head, the point grazing my temple. I cried out as I lunged for her legs, tackling her and bringing her to the ground.

"You have the right to remain silent," I said.

I may not have been a cop anymore, but I could always perform a citizen's arrest.

But before I could say more, a white light appeared next to us. Gertrude gasped and my breath caught. Hovering above the ground was a young woman that looked like Jane. She smiled at me and then in a blinding flash, she disappeared, leaving behind such a warm glow that peace spread through my chest, and I suddenly felt complete.

Justice had been served.

Twenty-six

·····································

INT. LIBRARY DAY

Georgia and Scott are seated in high-back chairs. Georgia's hair is curled softly around her face. She wears a lacy white top and lavender hip-hugger pants. Scott is dressed in a blue button-down shirt and slacks. His eyes are fixed on Georgia, doting on her.

GEORGIA
Hello, America. I know you've just been shown the confession reel from our killer. I'm happy to report to you Gertrude is in custody and is awaiting due process.

SCOTT
Thanks to you.

GEORGIA
Us. All of us. I can't take all the
credit. Without the amazing cast
and crew, I would have never gotten
close to figuring out who did it.
(lowers her eyes) And I'm sorry I
didn't figure it out sooner. I could
have saved some lives.

SCOTT
No, Georgia. Everyone makes their
choices. Those men sealed their fate
the day they turned their back on
Merle. *(pauses)* You do believe in fate,
don't you?

GEORGIA
(smiles) Definitely.

SCOTT
(stands up and pulls Georgia to her feet) You
have to believe. *(He reaches into his pocket
and gets down on one knee.)* Georgia, will
you make me the happiest man on earth and
marry me?

GEORGIA
(*takes his hands in hers*) I will. Oh, Scott.
I will.

Scott pops open the box and places the ring on Georgia's finger.
They kiss.

FROM *USA TODAY* BESTSELLING AUTHOR
DIANA ORGAIN

A First Date with Death

· **A LOVE OR MONEY MYSTERY** ·

Reality TV meets murder in the first in a new mystery series from the author of the Maternal Instincts Mysteries and coauthor of *Gilt Trip* from *New York Times* bestselling author Laura Childs's Scrapbooking Mysteries.

When brokenhearted Georgia Thornton goes looking for romance on reality TV, she has nothing to lose—apart from a good man, a cash prize, and maybe her life...

dianaorgain.com
penguin.com

M1731T0915

Connect with Berkley Publishing Online!

For sneak peeks into the newest releases, news on all your favorite authors, book giveaways, and a central place to connect with fellow fans—

"Like" and follow Berkley Publishing!

facebook.com/BerkleyPub
twitter.com/BerkleyPub
instagram.com/BerkleyPub